THERE IS GOLD IN EVERYTHING

There is Gold in Everything

Published by The Conrad Press Ltd. in the United Kingdom 2021

Tel: +44(0)1227 472 874
www.theconradpress.com
info@theconradpress.com

ISBN 978-1-914913-28-0

Printed and bound in Great Britain by Clays Ltd, Elcograf S.p.A

Typesetting and Cover Design by The Book Typesetters
www.thebooktypesetters.com

The Conrad Press logo was designed by Maria Priestley.

THERE IS GOLD IN EVERYTHING

Sam Coombes

Chapter 1

Y ou fall vertically through the air, your arms pressed against your side, your legs bound together by industrial strength string. The string is meant to attach to the parachute as you pull the cord; instead, no parachute escapes your backpack and the floundering string entangles around your legs as you fall.

Your arms are pressed against your side, your legs bound tightly together, a human arrow about to impale the land below. Well, that is your hope when in fact the reality is certain death approached at over two hundred miles per hour.

You will not impale the land. Your legs will break. Your pelvis will smash into a million pieces. Your daredevil spirit will extinguish in a second. Fortunately, your six o'clock morning alarm stops any of this excitement or inevitable pain and instead your morning routine begins.

Your cat has deadened your leg by laying on it at night and this has probably caused your dream that morning. You wash, clothe, and exit your house for the ten-minute walk to the train station. You think about the documentary you watched last night: there were some parts of India where the poor scoured sewers in search of gold. As strange as it seems, there are miniscule fragments of gold in the sewage systems that run beneath our streets. The hunt for wealth, the hunt for a different way of living, a better existence, this desire is within most, but is achieved by few.

What humans desire is a metal known on our planet to hold significant monetary value. One which is purchased when stock markets crash and relied upon to keep its value but is worth nothing in a world where money does not exist.

The physical presence of gold as it glistens, shines and draws you in to marvel at its wonder is merely a fleeting thought. On this wet and windy January morning you trudge wearily towards your train station. There is no gold, there is no shine and the attention that grabs you is a boring one. Your train is going to be seven minutes late. You stand there wet and annoyed and begin to think about a different world.

A world where you cannot sell the gold for money, nor use it to marry the one you love or indeed wear it as jewellery of any kind, because this gold exists only as a shiny metal, one of many special shiny metals.

You stand there, cold and miserable with your eyes closed, daydreaming about the warm fuzzy contentment experienced were you to find a large nugget of gold. The gleaming metal shines in your mind and as light reflects from this shimmering metal you begin to smile. You are happy.

The train station monitors flash once again. Your train is going to be another four more minutes. You close your eyes again. In your mind, you are surrounded by palm trees, sand and crystal-clear sea. A tear forms in your eye as you realise you are alone and the only thing to take you away from this lonely island is the breeze. You need to make a boat to get away from this magical, warm inviting island. Calm descends over your body as you drift into a deep, deep sleep on the platform bench. Your thoughts fade away into a dark and vacuous cave.

Sleep is your only way to truly relax and it is in many ways your saviour. For when you are awake the harsh reality that consumes every waking second is that you are alone, in a one bedroom flat, in the middle of small town you despise with only the odd tree to keep you company.

You crave nature, rarely seeing insects, no fish in the 'dead man's lake' nearby, not even birds seem to frequent the trees you do have. As each day passes in your mundane existence, you wish for more.

Sitting there at the station you close your eyes once more and visualise the crystal blue sea running away from the island you are standing on to reveal a bleached white landscape of nothingness. The seabed it leaves behind is barren, void of life and jagged with shells and stones moulded by the waves that once turned them. As you stare at this barren landscape in your dream, you look down at your naked body and focus on your feet.

You open your eyes. Your head is dipped down and you are looking at your feet. They are in shoes though and they are getting wet. Rain bounces off the platform floor. You look around at the dreary, sodden, grey concrete that surrounds you. It is dark, it is cold, and it is wet. You already know the train is going to be crammed full.

The doors open, and you give up without trying as everyone piles on and you walk on behind to find exactly what you expected. No seats available. The forty-minute journey is filled with people sneezing, snoring, sleeping and grunting.

You look around wondering how you ended up here; you had passed your eleven plus, you had spent seven years at a grammar school and then you had gone to university. A degree and then a Masters was sold to you by your parents as a way out of doing the jobs they had toiled over for over forty years each. Clearly, they were wrong.

Your mum worked in a potato factory and your dad stacked shelves in a warehouse. Both worked shifts and your childhood was spent dealing with your dad's mood swings and your mum's cheap, grey chicken which she said was, 'Just as good for you as that Marks and Spencer stuff'. They were hard working, honest parents and had a strict code of discipline at home, but that had not helped your sister. She ran away at sixteen and was pregnant at seventeen.

Mum cried for about two years before they reconciled their differences and became best friends during your sister's twenties. Your brother was ten years older and although you craved for his attention, his world revolved around himself. Staying at home till he was twenty-seven and with some healthy savings, he met a blond waitress and married her within a year.

That relationship did not last, and she now has three children from three different fathers, but at least it got your brother out of my parent's house and now he lives on his own. Still, he is OK, as he gets to see multiple women online and still manages to see his son on Sundays.

So, there is a brief diversion into family life, but you are still on this train wishing you were not here. Your friends are electricians, gas fitters, air conditioning salesman, PE teachers or London, city, money men all earning more than you. What do you do? You work as a youth mentor, helping young kids get away from their troubles and try to engage them in some productive enterprise.

For all your input and good intentions, you know that the hour you spend with each kid is outweighed by the twenty-three hours they spend with their gangs of friends in school, the dealers they meet out of school and their families which provide them with the attention of an iPad and a television.

Surely there is more? You get off the train and walk to your offices. The first smile of the day beams at you as you walk through the revolving doors to Janice, her long, blond, matted dreadlocks and bright pink vest top clinging to her ample breasts. 'Morning,' she exclaims in a bright and cheery voice. As you look in her direction, she has already turned around to talk to some-one else. You wish she paid you more attention.

Your morning joy of seeing Janice soon subsides as you scuttle to your desk to check your emails. There are various requests from local schools to visit various troublesome youths who have either been absent, arrested or involved in alcohol or drug abuse at an early age.

As you slump back in your chair you notice an envelope addressed personally to you sitting on your desk. A welcome surprise to your otherwise lacklustre day. You begin to open the envelope, not recognising the writing on the outside. It is not from your mum and you cannot think who else would write to you. As you hurriedly rip open the envelope there is an iridescent, somewhat transparent thin sheet of hard yet lightweight plastic. You notice a blank medieval font embossed on the plastic which reads:

Dear George,

Congratulations! You have been selected for a trip of a lifetime to Ridizing Island. The adventure begins on February 1st at Channel 49 offices in London at 9am where your itinerary will be relayed. Please come alone and be prompt. Bring with you a bag containing your passport, one white t-shirt, one pair of navy blue or black shorts and flip flops. Your bag will be checked for these contents and you will be flying to the Island that afternoon.

Best wishes,

Flamingo Productions

Your eyes immediately leap to your calendar to see it is Thursday the 28th of January. What are you going to do? You cannot remember entering a competition and you never entered anything online or in the newspaper. Then you recall the last thing you had entered was to win the two hundred and fifty gadgets from the gadget show competition, but that was about six months ago. What was this? Who were Flamingo Productions? Was it for real?

As you put the envelope on your desk, you look at it again for one more second before sliding it into your top drawer. You type Flamingo Productions into google and all that comes up are several garden furniture suppliers of plastic flamingos. You then type in Ridizing Island and again the search is fruitless. You then find the number of Channel 49 offices in London to ask about any shows or competitions involving Ridizing Island or Flamingo Productions.

A helpful lady called Suzi with a husky deep voice says she will ring you back. True to her word at 9:37 am your office phone rings and she apologetically says that no-one has heard of either Flamingo Productions or Ridizing Island. Your heart sinks as you think it must be some form of junk mail or a wind-up from one of your old school mates. The excitement it brings to your morning soon dissipates as you travel across town to an academy school where you are met by four youths at the entrance staring you up and down. You greet them politely, 'All right lads.' As you walk past the boys, they kiss their teeth and glare at you menacingly.

You quickly get into the reception area of the school and walk up to the reception desk: 'Hiya, I'm George Brittan from Youth Mentor UK. I'm here to speak to Abigail Lynch.' The receptionist grunts at you, 'She's not in today.'

The receptionist does not even raise her eyes from the magazine she is reading. She has dark black slick hair, stuck to her forehead, with dark eyeliner and her right eyebrow and left side of her upper lip pierced. You tap on the glass separating her reception room from the area you are standing in. 'Err, excuse me, yes, I'm here to meet a student, Adedoye Adekanye, and Abigail usually helps out.'

You wait for a response and the receptionist seems to take pity on you, 'Oh, sorry luv, do you still wanna meet him? Sign in here and put what company you're from and I'll ring through and see if he's about.'

Adedoye strolls towards you in a slow, loping, downtrodden way. He looks at the floor until he is within two feet of you and then looks up and nods subtly. Ade's school shirt is untucked, one of his shoes is not laced and he is wearing a tracksuit top which has stains on the left arm.

You greet him brightly, 'All right mate, how are you?'

You are upbeat and in your own buoyant way you try to show Ade that you have come to brighten up his day. He just shrugs his shoulders and replies, 'You know.'

As you walk with Ade back into the school towards the student services area, you talk to him about the envelope you received in the morning. He gives you his honest thoughts: 'Just junk.'

Ade spoke his mind and in your mind you tended to agree, but secretly you wish you were both wrong. As you sit down with Ade to catch-up on how his GCSEs are going your mind begins to wander as you dream of sandy beaches, scorching sun, tropical drinks and beautiful women…

'Sir!' Ade is shouting at you. As you blearily look up towards him he remarks, 'Sir, are you OK?' You reply, 'Yes, fine, why are you shouting?'

Ade looks to the ceiling in frustration, 'Sir, you've been asleep for like the past five minutes.' Embarrassed, you look around to check no adults are about and then apologise to Ade, 'Sorry mate, I had a terrible night's sleep and I'm just not with it.' Ade was kind, 'It's cool.'

You feel immense guilt realising what a great lad he is. You are the one person he trusts, and you have fallen asleep whilst he is talking to you.

'Ade, why don't I see if we can do something tomorrow afternoon.'

Ade looks a bit confused. 'What do you mean, Sir?'

You explain: 'Look, part of our mentoring is about celebrating your successes in school and your mock exams were great. I'm going to try and get you out of school tomorrow and we'll go to the West End and perhaps buy you an Arsenal top.'

Ade is quick to respond, 'Ah, man, that would be sick.'

Catching the momentum of his excitement, you say, 'OK, let me talk to a few people, whilst you wait here.'

As you wander the corridor to search for the Deputy Head, you notice posters on the wall with inspirational messages from famous people of the past and present. You spot Nelson Mandela stating, 'Education is the most powerful weapon you can use to change the world.' Then you see David Beckham saying, 'I look at myself every day and want to improve.' As you get towards a flight of stairs one poster grabs your attention, a Professor Spike Bucklow reflecting, 'Sometimes we're too clever to be wise.'

You begin to think about your car and the recent deaths from the polluted air in central London and realise how such a great invention, although clever, may not have been the wisest invention as the fumes suffocate the environment.

You look up the stairs and see a tall, slim figure of a man dressed in a three-piece suit wearing angular glasses and with wispy grey hair. You bellow towards him with confidence, 'Graham!' He instantly replies, 'Ssshhhh.'

Graham is a tall studious-looking man. He pushes his glasses down ever so slightly and presses his index finger against his lips before reprimanding you: 'Classes are still going on!'

You wait for him to get to the bottom of the stairs and then begin discussing Ade's recent achievements and the possibility of taking him out tomorrow. Graham replies, 'That should be OK, I just need to check his timetable and work commitments and I'll get back to you via email this afternoon.'

He is the Deputy Headteacher and has a firm and assured manner. He is a considered and erudite man in his fifties and appears far more relaxed when the bell rings and classical music starts playing in the corridors as the children leave their classrooms. You return to Ade and explain that the Deputy Head will be seeing him in the afternoon to confirm if you can meet tomorrow afternoon. You remind him to tell his parents too.

As you get back into your dented, navy blue VW Polo you notice a piece of paper on your passenger seat. You pick it up and notice the same medieval font that was on your letter this morning. It simply reads:

Don't forget to read your emails and contact Ade.

This is very strange as you have only just walked out of the school, so how could anyone have put that on the passenger seat before you had returned to the car. Then you second guess whether you had written it previously, but you are certain the car seat was empty having cleaned it in the morning before leaving the offices to school.

As you stop-start through heavy London traffic your mind begins to spin. The letter in the morning, the note on the passenger seat. What was going on? It must be one of your friends winding you up, so you text the usual suspects. Sean, a friend from when you went to secondary school, replies to you in his usual manner: 'Knob jockey!'

The reply from John Kraushaar, your friend for years from your local running club, is less condescending:

'Long time no hear, cowboy. Sounds like you've got another Bunny Boiler on your case, ha ha.'

It leaves you no option but to ring your parents, the dreaded phone call. They live in the same house, but don't talk to one another. They should have split up years ago, but who are you to talk when your own love life does not exactly shimmer like gold.

Your dad picks up the phone and gets excited when he hears your voice. As you relay the two notes from your office and the note from your car seat he laughs and says your memory is probably worse than his. He tells you that you have probably entered a competition without remembering.

You know this is not true as you never enter competitions, so ask to speak to your mum. She sounds genuinely intrigued and says she will do some 'digging' (her terminology for investigating).

As you get back to your office there are two people sitting in the waiting area. They appear to be a couple as the man has his hand on the lady's thigh. You ask, 'Can I help you folks?'

The lady stands up in a three-quarter length, grey, tailored pencil skirt clinging to her voluptuous behind and athletic legs. She is wearing a bright red pair of extremely high heels and extends her hand to you and grasps firmly before her sultry voice says, 'We've been waiting for you, doctor.' She pauses, 'We've always been waiting for you.' Her soft voice lingers. You stand confused, wondering why have they always been waiting for me? In a moment of bravery, you ask in a rather forthright manner, 'Sorry, what do you mean, you have always been waiting for me and why are you referring to me as doctor?'

At this point the man stands up quickly in a crisp black suit. He is tall and angular and stares through you with piercing, blue eyes. You think this is strange as his eyes do not match his springy, tightly curled, dark black hair.

'You are the chosen one and must come with us!' He is very 'matter of fact'. His dictatorial approach is far less accommodating than the sultry overtones of his colleague/wife/mistress or whatever their relationship is?

You assertively respond, 'Sorry mate, I've got a very busy day and I'm not sure what either of you are talking about. Have you checked in with Lynn at reception?'

As you turn to look at Lynn your face contorts as a zebra stares back at you in silence from behind the reception counter. You exclaim, 'What the hell!' You look back at the couple in complete astonishment. They just stare back at you motionless. The zebra's head, which was once Lynn's head, moves up and down and you stare at it again.

This time you are silently thinking, 'What the hell is going on?' You can't see Lynn so you look past the reception to your office and the white blinds which usually cover your window have been lifted. Your desk, computer and filing cabinets are all in order, but why are the blinds up? You can't remember pulling them up when you came in this morning? You look at the woman and ask her bluntly, 'What's going on?' She replies, 'We've come to take you away doctor.'

This is the third time they have called you a doctor. You start to feel angry about this whole weird situation and shout, 'Look, until you tell me what the hell is happening here, I'm not going anywhere.'

You feel yourself getting angrier and angrier and then suddenly there is an almighty bang and scream which forces you to the floor. Janice appears from a cloud of smoke screaming and you notice her breasts have two menacing-looking dark, coconut crabs attached to them. The crabs are waving their pincers frantically towards her face whilst their claws dig into her plastic, enlarged breasts. She runs past you and straight out the office door into the high street as you hear her wails drift off into the distance.

You turn quickly towards the sharply dressed woman and man and exclaim, 'I'm only going to ask one more time before I call the police. What is going on?'

Before they can answer you feel a mighty pain across the back of your head and fall to the floor.

Chapter 2

Whenever you went on holiday as a child you had a morbid fascination to find snakes. You would go out alone in the evenings, with your eyes peeled, along the seawall of some Mediterranean beach resort, hoping to see these slithering reptiles. You were often left feeling disappointed when all you came across was a fleet-footed lizard or two.

Although lizards still remind you of being abroad, because of the lack of wild reptiles seen in England, you still hope that on one balmy evening you will be able to see a snake. Now, as an adult, you are in Lanzarote on holiday with your wife. You turn to her one evening as you settle down to have dinner in an outdoor bar, 'Wouldn't it be great to see a snake!'

You are met with disdain, 'You are such a weirdo.'

Your wife then looks over her menu and says, 'What are you on about?'

You repeat your thoughts to your wife, 'You know, in England we don't see enough wild snakes and perhaps we might just glimpse one whilst we're abroad. We never have, but we might.'

The closest you come during the night are the lizards that run across the walls and ceilings of the bar you are sitting in, but never any snakes. Your wife looks at you as you gaze at them jutting in and out of the cracks in the roof. She laughs, 'You're soooo weird!'

This whole episode comes crashing through your mind as

you awake in an empty swimming pool filled with snakes. Your thoughts of lust for these reptiles soon disappear. You thought you would be fearless in such a situation. Wrong. Slithering, hissing, devil staring and gliding across one another you cannot move for the weight of a ginormous python which sits half coiled across your chest.

In a panic you try to inch your neck forward to survey the horror that confronts you, but you recoil quickly as a rattlesnake begins to display its distinctive warning. After 30 seconds of laying frozen you begin to feel the python move from your chest and the crushing sensation starts to subside as the giant eases itself away from your body.

You exhale, and as your chest sinks you take a sharp breath in, your chest expands up and you quickly sit upright to see a sea of writhing serpents. Green, brown, dark yellow and beige all coiling and twisting around one another. They look ominous. You look towards your legs and see them covered. In a burst of energy, you shake off the snakes to a crescendo of hissing and leap towards the side of the swimming pool.

As you shake your legs frantically once more, a man twice your size looms threateningly in front of you. He is wearing a black suit and white shirt holding a pistol against your forehead, pressing it so firmly you begin to bow as the gun is repositioned on top of your head. The enormous man addresses you belligerently, 'Going anywhere?' You cower and reply, 'No, no,' as you stand motionless in complete fear of your life being extinguished.

You are now looking at the floor with the hand pistol pressed on top of your head, but you notice the feet of another man appear. Navy blue suede loafers with tassels stand next to the shiny black shoes of the giant who has a gun against your head. 'Lo mollare,' says the man in Italian, which you vaguely understand to mean 'let go' because your wife had practised her language skills on numerous holidays. The pressure of the gun is released from the top of your head and as you look up you see two men, one the size of a gorilla with a shaved head and dark beard, his face looks distinctly Russian or of East European descent.

The other man with the blue tasselled loafers is wearing a white linen suit and navy-blue shirt but his face is shimmering in the light that reflects off the glass building behind the pool.

You cannot make out any of his features when suddenly you scream in utter agony as a snake sinks its fangs into your ankle. You crumble to your knees at the side of the pool and try to drag your body away from the snake pit. The man with the gun kicks away the snake back into the pool behind you. He wraps his hand around your forearm and you are dragged into a building nearby.

'Ottenere il medico,' shouts the man in the white linen suit and as the giant brute runs off you look at your foot and ankle which is twice its usual size and turning a dingy shade of green. He had shouted to 'get the doctor' and you begin to feel dizzy and nauseous as the man in the linen, white suit leans over you again. In pain you look up to him but cannot make out his face as the light shines through the large windows of what seems like a converted barn behind him. He doesn't appear to have a nose and his eyes look like small dots, but you are in such agony you don't care as your foot feels like it is about to explode.

After what seems like an age, a doctor appears and injects a syringe into your arm and another into your ankle. There is an immediate sense of relief that courses around your body and you feel completely relaxed and slightly euphoric. As the pain subsides your vision becomes less blurry and you notice the doctor walking out of the room you are now in and staring back through a window into the pool of snakes.

You watch him continue walking into another barn-type glass building at the far end of a courtyard which surrounds the pool you jumped out from. Suddenly you are slapped hard across the face by the large man who had held a gun against your head. 'You look where I tell you to look!' You lay there on the floor, head bowed and grateful to be alive. The man with the tasselled shoes stands between your legs and grabs the back of your head, pulling on your hair to force you to look up at him.

This time there is no doubting, he really doesn't have a nose. You look at two dots at the top of his face which look like holes and as he opens his small mouth to talk you notice he has no teeth and just a snake-like forked tongue. He sprays your face with saliva which stings your cheeks and lips as he begins to shout, 'Mi guardi di nuovo e il vostro morti.'

Unbeknown to you he has told you not to look at him, but you do not care and throw a wild punch which misses his oval shaped head. Before you can regain your balance the man in the black suit tackles you to the floor and as you try to grapple with him his superior strength overpowers you.

He flips you onto your chest before tying your wrists together tightly with plastic cable ties. You ask him to loosen the ties as the pain is excrutiating, but he just grunts at you.

As he gets off from your back the giant man grabs your ankles and begins to drag you along the flagstone, granite, grey tiles which begin to bump and graze your face. You try to lift your head but your chin catches a jagged edge and begins to bleed. Blood drips from beneath you and leaves a trail across what appears to be a large kitchen/diner area as you are taken into another room which is blindingly white.

The flooring is shiny white and the bottom of the walls are white too. Your legs are twisted around and as your hips follow the twisting of your legs, your shoulders and neck turn as you now look up to find a white ceiling. There is a large six feet by four feet window above you with the sun shining through directly into your eyes. You squint and feel yourself wanting to use your hands, but they are tied behind your back. You cannot block out the piercing sunlight which penetrates your eyes and reflects brightly around the shiny white room you find yourself in.

The giant East European man leans down towards your face and blocks out the sun before violently stuffing your mouth with a rag and tying it around the back of your head. You see him walk towards the only door of the room and leave. You lay there, unable to scream or talk and thankful you are still alive, when the man who had been speaking Italian appears directly above you on the roof of the building. He slithers his thin body through the window above you. Why is he up there? As you watch, you notice his head-shape change and flatten to squeeze through the tiny gap in the Velux window in the ceiling of this white room. You begin to wonder what he is going to do as the ceiling is about twenty feet from the floor and he has climbed through the gap in the window with his arm and head first. As he wriggles and slithers to get his hips through the 4 inch gap in the window, he falls rapidly towards you face.

You close your eyes quickly as you expect him to hit you at full force. You move your head sideways and keep your eyes closed, but there is no contact, no thud, no scream and you open your right eye slowly to notice the man is floating within an inch of your head parallel above your horizontal body. It frightens you deeply and your whole body tenses with fear.

You look directly into the black holes he has in place of eyes and an endless tunnel of darkness is flecked with gold. You feel an extreme weight across your chest but nothing is on you. You want to scream as you begin to feel your sternum cracking as this invisble pressure pushes harder and harder. You writhe on the floor in agony and notice your navy blue t-shirt is stained red with a circular blood patch, but an oily gold presence swirls like paisely print within your patch of blood.

The longer you look at your chest and focus on the gold swirls the less you feel pain. The man floating above you also begins to look at your chest; his forked tongue licks the swirling gold from your blood stained t-shirt and then quickly brushes his tongue diagonally across your face.

The gold burns and sizzles on your skin, but then this immediate pain quickly turns to a warm feeling, an erotic sensation, a pleasurable, euphoric, uplifting sense that overtakes your whole body. You have never felt so good as you feel the skin on your chin drawing together and sealing. The grazes and bruises on your face and ribs evaporate and you feel amazing. You can not make out what is happening as the man floating above you looks at your gagged mouth.

'Il tuo cuore è d'oro ora.' In a split second your gag disintergrates and so does the man. You do not know that this crazy creature had declared your heart as 'golden'. All you notice is the plastic ties on your wrists no longer exist, no marks remain, no bruises on your body, not a single blemish, and you stand up alone in this white room. As you look towards your t-shirt once more, you notice you are naked, no clothes and no hair on your body. You feel fresh, liberated and free when the door of the room opens and a huge giant of a man walks in and sees you standing there naked. He bows on one knee and says, 'Emperor, release me.'

You walk over to the man and ask him to stand up. 'What are you doing?' The huge man looks at you solemnly and replies, 'I am at your service, Emperor.'

Bemused, you ask, 'Well, tell me what is going on please?'

You do not care about being naked, you do not care about this giant man appearing to worship you. All you want is answers. As the brute stands up he says, 'You have been chosen as our next leader.'

Perplexed and really frustrated you retort, 'Leader of what. Who chose me?'

The giant man looks you straight in the eye and with his deep voice begins to talk. 'You are the leader of the land, the sea and the sky, you are Emperor and ruler of gold.'

By now you are so confused, 'This all sounds good, but where I'm from we've got a Prime Minister elected by the people. They try to govern the country so I'm not really sure how this Emperor malarkey works?'

The gargantuan Neandethal replies, 'There is no country, there is only land, sea and sky. You rule over us and we obey your every command.'

Chapter 3

As you walk past the man he drops to his knee and looks at the floor. You place your hand on the white door handle and as you push down the room changes colour to yellow and so does the man's shirt underneath his black suit. This amuses you and you walk out into the kitchen/diner area.

On the floor there are splashes of blood which appear bright yellow too. You walk out on the patio where all of the snakes inside the dry swimming pool appear in different shades of yellow, beige and light brown. The pool is at the centre of a courtyard and you wander over to the building directly opposite where you had been standing to an open door which is framed in wood and has glass panelling. You enter a room with wooden beams on the ceiling. There is a black, iron-cast chandelier and a long, dark, wooden antique table with at least twelve seats on either side. You are very confused and try to work out where you are when a woman dressed as a maid enters the room and immediately drops to the floor on one knee and bows her head.

You quickly grab your crotch and look for something to cover up your private parts. You look at the long table and behind three seats from the end stands a metal coat of arms. You wish it was a suit and in the time it took you to wish, you are wearing a yellow tailored suit which fits like a glove. You stand there feeling like a million dollars with matching yellow loafers with tassles like the ones you had seen on the man previously.

You see the woman looking at the floor and ask her to stand. Her maid's outfit of black and white turns to black and yellow and she appears bewildered and falls to the floor again. You command her to rise, 'Get up!'

After your command she stands and you ask her, 'Where am I?'

She replies, 'Italy, sir, you are underneath Italy.'

Confused you snap back, 'Underneath, what do you mean?'

She looks at you longingly with deep, dark, recessed eyes, 'The world is one now, Sir, and this land was once Italy but you have come to free us from the depths and bore us a new future through the undergrowth.'

Confused, you stand there momentarily trying to absorb what she has just said. 'Excuse me, did you say we are under Italy?'

The maid is quick to reply, 'Yes and you have been chosen to lead us to the promised land.'

You scratch your head in bewilderment,

'Errr the promised land? Where exactly is that?'

The maid now looks at you as if you have crushed her dreams with your ignorance, she then replies, 'But I thought you were King Guerrouj, son of Bobathamus.'

You like the thought of this, but realise honesty may be the best policy here.

'Mmmmm, well, sorry to disappoint, my name is George and I'm from Dartford, a forgotten town in England. And if you know about my town you'll know not many of us know our actual fathers.'

The maid looks at you disappointingly, 'Oh.' She pauses,

looking glum and then says, 'I guess you may not be the chosen one after all.'

As you look around in bewilderment you ask the maid how you got here. She quickly replies in annoyance that you do not remember the fact she had led you. She bursts out, 'Through the tunnels.'

You ask her to show you these tunnels. You leave the elongated room through the furthest exit. As you walk past the long table towards the door it slams shut behind you without any assistance. As it slams you hear thunderous laughter and jollity in the room that only seconds ago was empty, apart from you and the maid. You turn to her and ask, 'Who was that?'

She replies, 'What are you talking about?'

You persist, 'You know, all of the voices, the laughter and the clinking of glass as soon as we closed the door.'

The maid looks at you bemused, 'I don't know what you're talking about. Why don't you open the door to see?'

Cautiously, you turn around and gently, slowly push down on the door handle. When you feel the latch loosen you quickly push open the door. Nobody is in the room, however the table now hangs vertically suspended in mid-air with all of the chairs still in their position; but instead of being on the floor tucked-in horizonatally they are now hanging in the air with the table and are tucked-in vertically, suspended in mid-air.

You call over to the maid, 'Look!'

She doesn't respond and continues to walk away from you down a long and what looks like diminishing corridor. You chase after her leaving the door open, but as you run you notice the ceiling of the corridor getting lower and lower and now you are bent over with a crooked back and a C shaped curvature of your body. As you near the end of the corridor the maid turns around and says, 'Follow me.'

You continue to remonstrate with her, but she appears focused on moving forward and as she turns left through a door half your size you follow her into a pitch black room. You daren't move, frightened by the lack of light and the feeling of claustrophobia. Then you hear her soft, calming voice, 'It's ok. You can stand up tall.'

As you lift your hunched back you raise your hands but you can not feel a ceiling, 'Where are we?'

The maid is quick to reply, 'We are in The Connection.'

You feel uneasy and out of your depth with everything that has happened in the past 24 hours and start to panic. 'I can't see anything. How do we know where to go?'

She calms you immediatley. 'Just hold my hand, you'll be fine.'

You feel the soft, light touch of her delicate hand gently envelop your own as she begins to pull you slowly along the pitch-black nothingness before you. For around 5 minutes you walk in the darkness, blindly following the maid, hearing the occasional drip on the floor and the smell of damp in the air around you.

You tug on the maid's hand as a gesture to stop and as you kneel down to touch the floor it feels like hardened mud, the sort you had experienced before when you were a schoolboy cross country runner. Mud that had been compacted over time and was then moist through rain and dew. You run your left hand along the wall and can feel a bumpy, stony surface, reminding you of a castle wall.

As you come up from your crouched position you take two strides forward before the maid shouts at you to stop 'Ssshhhhh,' she says, as you imagine her pressing her straightened index finger to her pursed lips. You wonder why she has stopped. 'What is it?'

The maid pulls you forward and as you reach out you can feel three levers, each with a spherical end. The maid instructs you, 'I think we here.' She takes your right hand and guides it beyond the levers, and then says, 'Lay your palms flat.'

As you splay your hands flat beyond the handles you feel a cold, flat surface. You touch left and right and imagine there to be some sort of circular metal door in front of you. You picture a metal spherical door in your mind, one which could be similar to that of an entrance to a submarine. The maid instructs you again, she is urging you on. 'Place your ear against it.'

You press your ear against the cold metal surface and hear what sounds like water passing the other side. You are intrigued and ask, 'How do we open it without water rushing through and drowning us in here?'

The maid reassures you in her calm and eloquent voice,

'It's OK, there's a vacuum.'

Having failed physics miserably in school you just go with the tone of her voice suggesting that it's perfectly OK to open the door hatch. You pull down hard on one of the levers and feel a slight loosening before continuing to undo the entire hatch. As you open up the door your hope for some light evaporates and you expect to get wet, but nothing. You are instead met with the whirring and whooshing of water, but still in complete and utter darkness.

The eery, pitch-black water that surrounds you appears to be kept out by what feels to you like hard plastic as you clench your fist and knock on what is in front of you. As you walk forward the floor feels different and you reach down to feel a pebbled metal base similar to the metal drain slabs in the middle of roads. As you reach around you feel some sort of plastic-type material in a tube shape, a funnel perhaps, but there is nothing above your head.

The maid follows you in and you feel her crouch down slightly to close the hatch. She turns the internal levers which are located on the inside of the spherical metal door and you hear a clunk and click as the hatch locks. The maid then says, 'Don't be scared.'

Instantly you reply, 'I wasn't before you said that!! Is something meant to happen?'

You sense her bending down as her head bumps and brushes past your thighs. You feel her arm move downwards as her hand starts searching around your ankles until she touches the floor. You ask her, 'What are you looking for?' You sense the maid look up at you. She ignores your questions and replies, 'Here we go, just keep your arms by your side and tuck your chin in.'

As you feel her stand back she stamps on the floor and before you can talk you feel an enormous suction on the top of your head and shoulders. Remembering what the maid had said, you keep your chin tucked in and keep your arms by your side as you feel an enormous rush of air pass over your body. Within five seconds the darkness that has surrounded you begins to turn to light.

You feel a sense of relief as you are catapulted into the sky and the blinding, midday sun. As you wince you notice the vastness of the sea around you and then… splash. You land in the sea followed shortly by the maid.

You immediatley feel the weight of your tailored suit as it fills with water and you try to take it off as it clings to your body. The maid is quick to rid herself of her pinnifore and shoes. Soon you are both paddling to stay afloat with clothes bobbing around you. You ask the maid, 'Where are we?'

As you spit and splutter in the sea, you can just make out the outline of her body less than five feet away. Your vision is blurred through the water and hair over your eyes. As you look towards her you notice she has small black eyes and thick, dark mediterrean hair, lusciously lapping at her broad square sholuders. She replies, 'The Tyrrhenian Sea, I'm hoping you can swim.'

You're insulted, 'Yes, of course.'

She smiles, 'Good. Now follow me.'

You begin to follow her magnificent stroke. As she powers through the water you are astounded by her speed and grace. You breathe hard to keep up, but she is relentless and does not rest for what feels like an age. After around an hour of hard swimming you are exhausted. You ask, 'Where are we swimming to?'

She points in front, 'The Island. Come on, don't stop now, it is not far… it's now less than 10km.'

You feel yourself getting angry, 'What! 10km! That's miles away!'

She quickly corrects you in a sarcastic tone, 'Er, no, it's 10 KILO-METRES. Now, come on, stop moaning and start swimming.'

For the next three hours you swim continuously, stopping every so often to catch your breath. You start to daydream about all the swimming you had done as a kid. School galas, triathlon competitions and aquathons. You never thought they would lead you to this! Exhausted, you want to give up and then, from nowhere, you spot land on the horizon. The maid turns to you and shouts, 'Come on.'

She spoke in a relaxed manner as though she had just got back from a morning jog and decided to go for a dip. A fifteen kilometre dip! She is around ten metres in front of you. You think to yourself that she has not moaned once and so you have no right to either and continue to swim towards the land in front of you.

Each stroke feels weary and arduous as you drag yourself through the water. You have brief thoughts of sharks or man-eating predators beneath you, but care little as the exhaustion and tiredness consumes your body.

Finally you reach the rocky shores of an island which appears deserted. Your first thoughts are to find fresh water, but this basic need to survive is usurped by the outrageous, beautiful, shapely figure of the maid who climbs onto a rock nearby in just her thong and no bra.

She sits perched on the rock with her luscious, thick black hair slung over one shoulder and almost caressing her right breast. As you look up to her you shout, 'Are you OK?' whimsically hoping that she asks you to save her. When in fact you know perfectly well she is OK, but secretly wishing she needs some sort of comfort. She replies, 'I'm fine, but we must find some water to drink, I'm so thirsty.'

You clamber up the shore and across some rough tufts of

grass to a road. Beyond the road is a corn field and in the distance you can see a farm house. The sun is so hot and there is no breeze. As you look over at the maid, you point toward the house in the distance and she just nods as you both walk across the road towards a tractor track which cuts the field in two.

The maid covers her breasts with one arm as you both walk on the hardened mud beneath your feet which is cracked and dusty from the relentless sun that has been beating down on it all day. You brush your hands on the corn by your side and at once the whole field changes colour from green to a golden glistening yellow. The maid looks around her as swathes of golden leaves glisten under the midday sun. She looks at you and says, 'You still don't know, do you?'

You look back. 'Do you want to tell me what is going on?' She nonchalently shrugs her shoulders and looks completely nonplussed as she ups her pace towards the farmhouse.

You don't want to be behind her for fear of being caught oogling at her pert derriere, so quicken to walk along by her side, slighlty in front. As you approach the farmhouse you notice the white, tattered boarding is slightly rotted underneath the sash windows. The tiles on the roof look broken and a stray dog runs straight past you as you approached what appeared to be a dilapidated building.

As you came closer, a gust of wind blows across your face and you hear doors creaking. You became transfixed by a small paper windmill fluttering furiously in a plant pot next to the front door. You suddenly feel uneasy and this sense of fear can be seen in the eyes of the maid who ushers you to knock on the front door. The faded, dark green door smells of stale urine and as you knock there is a loud bang from behind the door.

You both step back and then suddenly the door flings open and whacks against the wooden-clad house. An old man with a wispy white and grey beard stands before you. He looks dishevelled, unshaven and he is wearing a white vest with holes in it and trousers which look dusty and worn. A piece of rope is tied around his waist, clearly keeping his trousers up, and his feet look thick and bulbous with cracked skin all around his heels.

'Che cosa?' asks the man in an aggressive forthright tone. The maid looks at the man with credulous eyes and dry white streaks of sweat around her face. He has uncompromisingly asked, 'What?' She speaks only one word and it is obvious to see in her foamed mouth that she is in distress. She pleads, 'Acqua.'

The exhaustion has caught up with the beautiful maid and she places both hands in front of her in a begging plea to the farmer. The old man looks confused and then ushers us both into his home with a bear-like hand.

As you walk into his home there is brass paraphernalia hanging from all the walls and very low, misshapen ceilings. You duck under a wooden beam into his kitchen. The old man gives you a large, white mug and as you hold the mug to your mouth it immediately turns yellow. The man looks at you in astonishment.

'Esci!' he bellows, as he points to his front door, pushing you in the back. It is very clear he wants you out of his house. The maid is pleading with him in Italian for water, but he just keeps shouting, 'Esci, esci.'

As you are frog-marched out of his home you glimpse some heavy, cropping machinery equipment in a side garage. The angry man slams his front door and you quickly get the maid's attention, signalling to her to head towards the big garage where you can see tractors and other heavy machinery.

You place your index finger against your lips and cower slightly as you scurry across an open courtyard to the garage. You look around praying to find a container with some water in it. You then start to contemplate drawing water from one of the engines of a tractor or combine harvester. The search becomes a panic and as you look around frantically you begin to feel faint as your vision becomes blurred. Your legs become weak and unsteady before you hear a soft but firm, instruction, 'Prescelto.'

You stumble in her direction and notice she is pointing towards an outdoor tap dripping in the corner of this giant garage. As you kneel, you ask for her to turn on the tap as you have no strength left in your arms. She calls you the chosen one as you had saved her life without even knowing.

You lay under the tap as it gushes into your mouth and around your face. You feel the water swirling down your throat and into your body and you feel saved. The sense of relief is palpable. The maid joins you under the tap and you look at each other with knowing eyes. You only just survived. As you stare at one another you decide to question the maid, 'What is your name?'

She replies in perfect English, 'Just call me maid.'

You do not press her on this as you are too exhausted. 'OK, well, maid, we need to get out of here before that angry farmer finds us.'

She nods and then jumps quickly behind a tractor. You are taken aback with this action and then you hear an almighty tearing sound from behind the tractor and she reappears with tarpaulin draped over her.

Although slightly disappointed not to be able to see her beautiful body, you acknowledge her finding some form of clothing and nod towards her in agreement. You do the same and cover your body with some material; you get an inner warmth and feeling of comfort as the material wraps around your torso.

The maid points to a back door and as you place your hand on the handle the door begins to turn yellow. Before long, the whole corrugated metal garage begins to turn from a dark, dusty grey to a vibrant, shiny yellow. You shout at the maid, 'Quick!' She looks all around her in amazement, but you just want to get away and tell her to do so, 'Hurry, we need to get out of here, this isn't funny.'

You do not know what is happening and run through the door and as the maid follows, you both enter another cropped field where a line of trees can be seen on the horizon. You point to the trees and exclaim, 'We'll run to there and then rest up when we're out of sight from this farm and that crazy farmer!' You feel very tired and sluggish as you jog through the field to a line of cypress trees. You never look behind and just hope the farmer has not followed you.

As you near the trees you see a long, straight road splitting the landscape and disappearing into a mountain range ahead of you. The maid, who looks just as tired as you, wearily whimpers, 'What are we doing?'

You have a plan in your mind and swiftly reply to her, 'We

are going to walk along this road and hitch a ride to the mountains. Once we get there, I think it's about time you start answering some of my questions and tell me what the hell is going on.'

She shouts back at you, 'Me! You're the one who is meant to come and save us, you need to tell me what is going on!'

You slow down and start to walk together. You explain to the maid about the strange envelope on your desk and the people at your office. Your colleagues turning into zoo animals and the pain in the back of your head before awaking in a pool of snakes.

The maid listens intently as you walk together along the road. She then begins to laugh, 'You should be a storyteller, that's hilarious.'

You look at her with an annoyed face and say, 'No, honestly, that is exactly what happened.'

You could tell the maid did not believe you and you felt there was no point trying to convince her considering your current position. She turns to you and shows you a half-hearted belief in her response, 'OK, OK, whatever. Let's just get to the top of the field and follow your plan and see where that gets us. Hopefully, I won't turn into a giraffe by then!'

The maid started laughing to herself and you began to see the funny side as the whole situation did appear rather surreal. Nevertheless, you had a niggling suspicion that the maid must know more than what she was letting on as she had been in the house where the snakes occupied the swimming pool.

She was in the vicinity when the men were aggressive and eerie. She had led you to wherever you had ended up. So, she must know something. You stop thinking about it as you reach the top of the field. You can see three trees separated from the others and the maid appears to be gesturing towards them. She points at the trees, 'Come on, let's take a break by those three trees. I'm starving, aren't you?'

You sit beside one another, alone in the top left-hand corner of a ploughed field which is adjoined to acres and acres of fields with no one in sight. You feel a bit more relaxed knowing you are out of sight of the farm below. The sea sparkles in the distance and you turn to the maid and reply, 'Yep, I'm famished, but this is a beautiful spot to rest, just look at sunlight reflecting off the sea.'

The maid ignores your sentimental words again and says, 'I am sure it is the first tree.'

You look up at her prodding and pushing against the Cypress tree. 'What are you doing?'

It looks odd to you as she continues to inspect the first tree in the cluster of three. As you look on the floor you notice the raised roots of the tree protruding from the ground. There appears to be raisins or rabbit droppings amongst the crevices in the roots. In the vain hope they are raisins and, in your delirious and starving state, you pick up a handful ready to eat. As soon as they touch your palm, they turn into tiny nuggets of gold.

You turn to the maid and open your hand. As the gold glows in the evening sun you ask again, 'What is it with this tree?' She lets out an anguished scream in a frustrated state and bellows, 'No, nothing, it must be the second.' You have no idea what she is searching for but follow her to the second tree of the cluster, three metres away.

The second tree looks windswept and lifeless. In contrast to the first tree this second bore no leaves, no fruit and appears lifeless with faded twigs and branches. The tree seems vulnerable with the large branches looking ready to snap at any point. You kneel again on the ground, this time it is dusty; the dust feels like the most refined sand you have ever touched. You say to the maid, 'Soil seems different here, but we're only a couple of metres away from the other tree.' As you pick up a handful of this dusty sand, it slides through your fingers.

The dust grains in your hand fly off in the wind and as you watch them, they sparkle, glisten and shine forming a shimmer of golden sand which falls quickly at the base of the tree. The maid appears to be looking longingly at the tree and catches you staring at the golden dust mound by its base. You ask her, 'And here?' hoping she believes this tree to be special after what you had just witnessed with the dusty sand. A big gust of wind flurries across your face and stirs the loosely wrapped tarpaulin off from the maid's body.

She screams, 'It cannot be!' and reaches out to a branch, to steady herself, that snaps into her hand. As she falls to the floor, her hand bleeds onto the dusty surface. You rush to her aid but stop in your tracks to stare intently at the droplets of her blood begin to mix with the small mound of dusty gold at the base of the tree.

Her blood and the golden dust begin to rise together into the air before splattering against the trunk of the third tree. You both stare in astonishment, pause, look at one another and then march authoritatively towards it. The maid shouts excitedly, 'It must be!' She continues to lie strewn across the floor whilst pointing at the sparkly gold in her blood now running down the bark of the final tree.

You kneel for a third time next to a sprawling entwinement of thick exposed roots. The ground looks wet this time and thick with mud. The mud appears black, a mysterious black, not dark brown, nor dark like wet mud, but black. You stand about 2 feet away from this black mud surrounding the exposed roots, just staring.

Then in a moment of courage you plunge your hand into the mud. The slimy consistency consumes your arm and you feel your whole arm being pulled further beneath the roots. You try to resist and in no time your entire arm, up to your shoulder, is beneath the mud. You look towards the maid, 'I think I'm in trouble here.'

They are your last words before a rapid jolt pulls your whole body into a thick darkness. You close your eyes and hold your breath, but within a second you feel able to move your arms. As you spread them, you open your eyes. Two angels a tenth your size flutter in front of you. The first angel flutters towards your face and speaks, 'Hello, I am Rose.' And then the second angel comes closer, 'Hello, I am Dandelion.'

As the angels flutter before your face you notice you are suspended in what you can only think is an underground cave. All around are flecks of gold glimmering in the darkness that surrounds you. You float in a cloudy haze and as the angels flash past your face, streaks of light cut through the mist and you see gold. You ask the angels, 'Why am I here and who are you?'

The angels are both green and one flutters with pink flowers on her head whilst the other flutters with pink flowers on her feet. They speak in unison, 'We are your friends and we are here to help you discover you.'

That doesn't make sense, so you ask, 'Discover me?'

They reply again in unison, 'Yes.'

You tell them curtly, 'I know who I am, thank-you very much, but I have never met an angel before.'

The angels look at each other and then straight back at you.

The angel with pink flowers on her feet replies, 'Do not be alarmed, I am Rose and I am what you think people think of you.' Confused, you look at the other angel who you hope will give you some clarity. The second angel just looks at you nonchalantly and says, 'And I am Dandelion and I am what you think you are.'

Your brain spins at their philosophical jargon, 'Er, OK, whatever you say.' You then ask, 'Can you now tell me what I am doing hovering beneath a tree with two fairies in the dark surrounded by mist speckled with pieces of gold?' The fairies look at one another and then suddenly stare upwards at the sprawling roots of the tree.

You follow their gaze and look upwards at the dangling roots which hang motionless in the pink swirling haze that surrounds you. As you stare at the roots you see two come towards your face, except they are not roots, they are legs. They are the legs of the maid who started to appear above your head as though the roots of the tree were giving birth to her. She flips her body through a transverse plane so that her head is now pointing towards yours and she begins to use breaststroke to move through the haze.

The fairies hang in the midst next to you and stare with loving eyes as the maid comes closer. As she approaches, the maid turns to you and answers the question you had posed to the fairies. 'We are here George, for you to use gold for its original purpose.'

You are confused and ask, 'Er, OK, what are you talking about?'

The fairies turn to the maid and Rose says, 'Are you sure this is the right man?' The maid is adamant in her reply,

'Definitely!' She quips, 'Just look at his nose.'

You touch the front of your face and squeal, 'My nose!'

As you brush your hand over the space where your nose used to be, you can feel slight flares in the middle of your face where your nose once was, but no protruding nose. Your mind quickly goes back to the men at the house. Their facial features are now your own. You realise you have not looked in a mirror since leaving that strange place and hadn't really touched your nose. Perhaps that was why the farmer wanted you out, albeit you had turned everything you touched into yellowy gold.

You then begin to breathe heavily, confused and upset with these changes to your body that you didn't even know had occurred. As you breath, you notice each intake of breath is not air, but something a little thicker and containing tiny stone-like particles, which shoot up your nostrils on every breath but cause no pain, just a tingling sensation in your spine.

Not only has your face changed without you noticing, but so have your senses. Your vision seems sharper as you notice minute details on the anther and stigma of the miniscule flowers attached to the feet of the fairy, Rose. As you place your hand on your face again, you notice your eyes seem smaller, a lot smaller, but your visual acuity is immense. You scream at everyone around you,

'What has happened to my face?'

Dandelion mockingly replies to you, 'My gorgeous friend, you are even more beautiful!' Her joke continues,

'We heard a tall, dark handsome man would come to save us, but you are taller and more handsome than we ever imagined.'

Rose is staring at your chest and arms. She continues Dandelion's praise, 'And your physique!'

You feel your left bicep with your right arm and even you are impressed. You then feel your right arm with your left hand and begin to smile. Looking down at the veins in both biceps you notice your arms look pumped and your whole torso appears visibly ripped. You are energised. The maid stares at you knowingly and says,

'Come on, we've got work to do.' As she grabs your hand you feel strong and this surge of power courses around your body.

The maid begins to swim deeper into the cave as you hear the fairies wishing you good luck. The fear you felt when entering this place had turned to a sense of adventure and you feel exhilarated.

You ask the maid, 'Where are you taking me?'

She replies meaningfully, 'Deep, deeper than you've ever been before.'

You think about this for a second and ask quizzically, 'Before?'

She replies, 'Yes, you've been here before, but only in your mind. Now this is reality and we're going to the cuore of the gold.'

You think you have misheard her, 'What do mean?' You pause for a response and repeat, 'What does cuore mean?'

She enlightens you, 'The heart.'

The maid then repeats herself, 'We're going to the heart.'

As you swim deeper down into the thick hazy mist, the specks of gold that once glistened around the roots of the tree begin to fade. You start to feel colder as the maid's grip becomes tighter around your hand. She looks startled as she says, 'Look!' She points in front of you towards a distant smoky glow. You can feel the maid's excitement as her breaststroke swimming motion started to quicken towards the glow and she let go of your hand.

You are momentarily frightened, 'Wait, wait!' You are consumed by the complete fear of not knowing where you are or what you are doing. The glow begins to brighten, and the mist starts to clear; before long you are wincing at the intense light emanating from what appeared to be some sort of creature. It is small and motionless on what appears to be a leaf. Both are gold and appear to be vibrating at an incredible speed.

You shout at the maid who appears hypnotised in bewilderment, 'Maid, snap out of it.' But as she looks back at you, her eyes change. Two black horizontal stripes cross the centre of her eye. She looks directly at you and says in an ominous tone, 'Now is the time.'

You look at her, 'For what?' shortly followed by you telling the maid, 'You look crazy!'

She grabs your hand and forcibly explains, 'You have been chosen. You must take the bee from the leaf and make it go to work. The world as you know it is unbalanced and it needs you to turn the tide, literally.' Her emotional plea is confusing and you query her intent, 'Sorry, I am completely lost. What are you going on about?' Quick as a flash she responds, 'Just grab the bee.' She appears agitated and angry, pointing towards the vibrating insect. As you reach down to clasp the bee, the leaf on which it is lying shrivels and turns a pale brown. It immediately evaporates into a million tiny microscopic pieces.

The maid commands you in a panicked tone, 'We must leave immediately. Quickly, follow me.' You swim with the bee still vibrating in your hand and follow the maid further into a dark passage. She turns to you and says, 'You need to hold your breath now.' In the darkness you can only make out the outline of her body as the maid stops abruptly and begins to kneel. You ask, 'Are you on the floor?' You try to touch the ground but cannot feel anything and cannot understand how or why she is kneeling. Her chin is tucked into her chest and as she looks back in your direction her eyes have changed once more. They are now illuminous white, and her face has taken on the colours of the horizontal stripes; she is a black, dark vacuous black.

The maid turns to you with her glowing eyes and exclaims, 'I will light the way, you must follow me quickly as what you have known is collapsing. Very soon you must hold your breath and trust me.' Her eyes light the surrounding nothingness and all you see is black, everywhere is black. Then, as you drift by her side following her every move, you make out what appears to be mirrors of tree branches, twigs and leaves.

The mirrors begin to crack as the maid looks at them with

her beaming eyes. They shatter loudly and shards of mirrored glass fly past your head which you hold to avoid being hurt. You are anxious and cry to her, 'Where are we going?' Your fear becomes a terror and you desperately try to stay close to the maid as the thick black surroundings start to play on your mind. The only thing that keeps you sane is the trust you have for the maid. She turns to you with her bright white eyes, 'Reality has changed; we're heading back inside the tree to the top. Now don't stop and stay close to me.'

She is firm and sees you are scared. She swims straight through the shattered mirrored glass and her eye beams reflect and bunce around like lasers in a nightclub. Then the mirror reflections stop and all you can make out through her vision are branches, twigs, and leaves.

As you approach them you cover your eyes and they scratch your body and poke and prod at your abdomen and legs. You hear the maid making noises ahead of you as she breaks through more branches until she stops to turn to see where you are. She shouts back at you, 'OK, now, when I pull on the top of this branch it will cause your reality to shatter. Water will rush out from where I am at the top of this tree, hang onto any branches nearby and whatever you do, don't let go of the bee! After the initial rush of water, there will be calm, and you will sense a steady flow. You need to swim against that flow and into the trunk of a tree. When you are inside don't stop swimming and head towards the light. The light is the surface of the water.'

You nod and then watch as she counts down on her left hand, three fingers, two fingers then one finger and then a vicious pull with her right hand on a lever type branch you can not make out. Everything around you does not shatter, it melts as hot water bursts right through the darkness leaving you swirling in an intense scorching stream. You are battered by the water and it stings all your exposed skin whilst you try desperately to keep your eyes open.

You can just make out the maid flailing around, hanging onto a thick protuberance of wood. After around ten seconds the water flow calms and you immediately become cooler. You quickly swim towards the light in front of you. You are swimming unwittingly towards the maid's eyes and as you get near to her face she points towards a flow of water on her right. You are rushed along by the current of a stream which leads you down inside of a tree. As you hit the floor, water surrounds you and you begin to float upwards inside the trunk.

You see sunlight above and the water around you begins to steam and evaporate. The heat is excruciating, and you climb the inside walls of the tree. As you climb upwards you burst through a seal and take a huge inhalation of air.

Before long, the maid appears by your side and immediately you say, 'Am I pleased to see you!' Your rhetorical statement puts a smile on her face as she replies, 'That's the spirit. I hope you've still got the bee?'

You are proud to open your clenched fist and reveal the bee, 'Yep, check it out.' Your sense of accomplishment at keeping the bee alive and surviving the whole surreal experience makes you feel amazing. The maid's eyes glisten green and she says, 'We've just begun; now follow me.'

Chapter 4

As she starts to swim you notice the blue skies start to cover with cloud and they become darker and darker. In front of you, less than 100 metres away, is a ginormous cliff face, but as you swim towards it, the current drags you away.

It seems to take an age to get to the shore and as you look up towards the imposing cliff face, the first thing you notice is it stretching endlessly both left and right, like a huge white wall of chalk. The nearest recollection of such a cliff face is that of the white cliffs of Dover or the enormity of El Capitan in Yosemite Park, America.

The dark clouds above caress and bounce along the tops of these huge, dreary, lifeless-looking cliffs. The whole place is deathly silent. The maid breaks the atmosphere as she speaks: 'We are here. Now release the bee.'

The shore you are standing on is grey and full of slate-like stones mixed with depressing, black, ash-like sand. The whole place is desolate, eerily quiet apart from the slushing sea upon the shore. There are no birds, no seaweed and the cliff faces look bereft of life.

The maid looks straight at you as she speaks: 'You know we are at the bottom of the bottom. You have travelled to a new dimension of your own reality; we have arrived at the bottom of the ocean and the water you see is merely a reflection in your mind. The real world lies up there beyond the clouds.'

You have no idea what she is talking about. 'So why are we

here?' The maid responds, frustrated at your lack of understanding, 'Because you have to disrupt the way.' Still you have no idea. 'The way?'

She explains: 'Yes, you have been chosen as a light amongst the darkness, as a soul amongst the soulless, as a visionary, a leader who can turn the world as we know it on its head.' She pauses, 'I mean literally, turn it.' She looks at you with her eyes now appearing to be double in size and quite scary. They have changed once more and now shimmer red with gold flecks of fire in them. She summons you with conviction: 'Now release the bee. Watch as the World around us turns on its axis' You don't understand. 'What do you mean?'

She replies sharply, 'When you let go of that golden bee its vibrations will multiply a thousand times and then a thousand times more. The bee will replicate itself over and over again as you have released it from its power source, the golden leaf. You will not be able to recognise the bee, as it will become a wave of gold that cuts through the land and when it does you must fly with this golden army to lift the land and disrupt the life above it. Every land mass in this world needs to be tipped, it needs to be re-aligned and placed on its side. This will submerge much of existence as you know it. Mountains will fall, rivers will run dry and forests will drown. But you must cleanse the world, shake up existence and let nature take over again.

'Civilization as you know it is about to die. What you have in your hand is the key to unite a new world. As the land is cut from beneath the feet of the people that live on it, the ensuing chaos will bring people together, new people. Those who survive will have to do so together in an entirely new environment for people to co-exist and start again.' She pauses, 'Now................... release the bee. Aaarroooozzzzzzeeeeeeeggggaaaaaaaaaa!'

You hesitate to digest what she has just said and consider the massive implications. Your mind then flashes to your boring Tuesday afternoon meetings with your boss Graham. All he ever did was drone on about the need for everyone to do their Health and Safety training and you think out loud, 'Yeah, let's live a little. If she's speaking the truth and if I'm not in some sort of hallucinogenic dream then this is sure going to mix things up a bit!' As you let go of the bee it flies in a direct, straight line towards the cliff leaving bee after bee behind it. As each replica appears, the whole line of bees starts to extend from front to back and as the first bee buries its head into the cliff, it creates a whipping effect on all the bees behind which begin to wrap around the base of the cliff.

You witness a thin golden line at the base of the rock growing longer and longer until you cannot see the base joining to the ground. It has been replaced by a thin golden line stretching for eternity left and right.

You turn to the maid. 'Now what?' She replies instantly, in a soft tone, 'You must wait.' As the bees burrow deeper and deeper into the rock the golden line they form becomes harder and harder to make out. The glinting bees begins to disappear into the rock face. The maid can see you are squinting and says, 'Use your eyes.' You are using your eyes, so you reply, 'What do you mean?'

Her red flame-filled eyes bulge as she raises the pitch of her voice, 'You have the power. You are no different to me and can illuminate the darkness, but first you must believe.' You are annoyed at her reply, 'You talk in riddles, what are you talking about.'

She takes your hand and walks you closer to the rock face. The golden line is now invisible as it is too deep into the rock surface. The maid looks at you, 'Rise up.'

As she says it you feel your feet lift from the ground and look at her, 'What's happening?'

In your head, you have wanted to rise, because you are desperate to see along the line of bees. You want to fly left and right along the cliff face to see what is happening. What were the bees doing to the cliff? Then, as you are thinking all of this, your feet leave the ground.

The maid grabs your hand, squeezes it tight and then softly, slowly releases her grip, and you rise higher and higher as you speed left and right along the cliff face, the crack now appearing dull but just visible in front of you. In desperation to see more you shout, 'Illuminate!'

Your eyes shine a bright white light through the minute crack in the cliff. You see deep into the cliff. Around 50 metres ahead of you, buried deep inside, you see the golden bee line reflecting your white laser-piercing vision of light from your eyes. The maid floats next to you and says encouragingly, 'That's it.'

She stirs your emotions and makes you feel invincible. Urging you on she says, 'You must entirely believe. Your strength will come from that belief.'

You slowly turn to the maid, 'I want to get closer.'

Her eyes burn intensely as she furiously snaps back, 'No, the bees are busy doing what they do. You cannot disturb their work; it is essential they complete the task at hand.'

You are alarmed at her seriousness, 'How will we know when they are done?'

The maid looks at you with a fixed stare and calmly says, 'You will know. You have led them here and you will continue to lead them. Do not be afraid, they belong to you.'

You drift with the maid back down to the dark, grey black sand and shale beneath you. As you drift down you are perplexed by what the maid just said. 'What do you mean afraid?'

The maid replies, 'When over a billion bees fly towards anyone, people are usually afraid.'

You think she makes a fair point, 'Oh, right.'

And with that you notice the floor begin to tremor and the waves become ever more violent out at sea. The shale and sand beneath your feet quiver and quake and you hear a roaring murmur. It becomes louder and louder and louder until you are covering your ears in pain at the noise.

As you look up towards the clouds above the cliff, the sky begins to fill with a swarm of golden bees and then you know. The maid is screaming at you as the swarm approaches, sounding like a jet engine coming directly towards your face. You can hardly make out what she is screeching in your direction: 'Stay still!' You look up at this huge cloud which begins to break and spike towards you. Instinct takes over and you scream back, 'No way.'

You start to run down the beach, not knowing where you are going as you feel the wind swirl and get stronger behind you. You dare not look behind but can not resist and, as you peak over your right shoulder, a line of golden bees appears to be chasing you down.

They are falling from the sky like gannet birds diving into the ocean for fish. They accelerate so quickly and from the clouds they come down in golden streaks towards the maid. She stands motionless as they veer past her head and start coming towards you. The maid shouts to you in hopelessness desperation: 'Put out your hand!'

Having followed all her advice so far, you thought it prudent to continue. Whilst still running away up the beach you hold out your right hand behind you, as though you are about to receive a baton in a relay race. There is an almighty thud as your hand is struck in the centre of your palm and then a flurry of hard strikes continued unrelenting.

You slow to a jog and your heartbeat begins to drop as you suspiciously look down at your hand. You can make out a golden bee, viciously vibrating whilst other bees fly straight into it and are absorbed immediately. As more and more bees come into your hand, the vibrating becomes more violent and you decide to close your hand into a fist.

You stop moving and the bees now work their way into your clenched fist from both ends, attacking the small hole inside your curled index finger, wrapped by your thumb. The bees merge into each other but don't grow or enlarge. They enter both ends of your fist as you clench it firm, squirming their way into your hand and uniting with the bee you were holding firm.

You can feel the bees quivering and fidgeting to get into your hand, but as it was now closed more and more bees start to land on top of your clenched fist, trying to find a way to get inside. Soon it is as though you have a giant hive covering your right arm. You start flapping your arm up and down, but this does nothing to deter the bees and more keep coming from the sky and down the beach towards you.

In a panic, you start to run again, and a few bees fall from your arm. You think to yourself, 'I know, I'll run into the sea'. The bees that are clinging to your arm immediately let go and you feel instant relief. As you peer down the beach you can see the maid running in your direction.

The bees are now following her but not landing on her. As she comes closer, you can see her waving her arms frantically, 'No, no, you can't!' She is shouting from the shore. 'You must get out and let the bees return home. We need all of the bees otherwise the strength of the one you hold diminishes.'

You look glumly towards the maid who now has hundreds of thousands of bees swirling around her head in a thick cloud. You know deep within you that she is only trying to help, so you glumly walk back out from the sea. As you wade back to shore, you open your hand to look at the bee: it has turned a bluey grey colour and has stopped vibrating so vociferously. Within a second of you noticing this another bee divebombs into your hand, then another and another.

You look down and the bee begins to change colour; its original golden glow begins to return and as more bees hit your palm the glow gets brighter and the vibrations get stronger. You close your fist and the maid smiles at you as she says, 'Stay calm. The bees do not want to harm you, they are here to help, they are here to bring life. Relax and let them come home.' You look at the maid and she looks right back at you. 'Now sit down and cross your legs and hold out your palm. Close your eyes.'

As you copy her actions, you sink into what appears to be

some sort of yoga pose. You notice the bees begin to drop from the sky like rain drops into your palm and before long they feel like cotton wool. Keeping your eyes closed you ask, 'Why are they changing, why do they feel different?'

The maid opens her eyes which now shine gold. She speaks softly, 'They are you.' The maid then closes her eyes and continues to speak, 'Your energy is their energy. As you relax, they relax. Now, let them come home. Ssshhhhhh.'

You imagine the bees massaging your palm and begin to drift off into a dream-like state as you sit cross legged on the beach. Eventually you feel nothing in your hand and awaken abruptly knowing the importance of the original bee. It is sat there in the palm of your hand, vibrating thunderously, but you feel nothing. You imagine the bee's immense power and look over at the maid who is sat in a trance 5 metres along from you on the beach. You holler towards her, 'Heelllllllllllooooooooooo!' She opens her left eye first and then her right, and you ask, 'Err, now what?' You bow your head towards the single bee in your palm. The maid looks at you, and you look again at the bee to draw her attention to it.

The maid looks up at you and says, 'Now the line has been made, you must move the land.'

You look up at the enormous, never-ending cliff face and reply sarcastically, 'Yeah, yeah, you mean now we've got the easy part of toppling an entire country on its side!'

The maid ignores your sarcasm, 'First you need to get into the centre of the island. Once you are there you must release the bee. It will multiply once more and will join forces with you as you carry the island on your back. Just like Atlas from Greek mythology carried the world on his back, now it is your turn. Hahahahahaha.'

You are not impressed by her laughter and look at her solemnly. 'You're joking, right?'

She glares at you. 'Look, George, you have been chosen to shake things up. You don't yet believe this and yet you have hovered in the sky, swam beneath a tree, travelled through the depths of the ocean. I mean, what more do you want?' The maid looks exasperated and you take her points on board. Plus, it was the first time she had referred to you by name. This time her comments felt personal.

'OK, OK, so now that the bees have scarred the core of the country how do we, or, more pertinently, how do I, lift the island to turn it on its side?' The maid looks at you and shrugs. 'It's about time you start leading the way around here, because after this country you've got over a hundred more land masses that need turning.'

You look up at the rock face and, where the bees had once penetrated along the surface of the rock, you can see a thin, dark grey line with specks of gold. The maid looks at you and can sense your quizzical gaze. She says,

'They didn't make it out in time before the land fell again.' You want to look more closely at the line and as this thought crosses your mind your body begins to rise from the ground. You drift along the beach to look closely at the scarred rock face.

You begin to fixate on one of the glinting, gold specks and as you drift closer you can see a bee caught between rocks, dirt, stones and earth. The bee is twisting and turning violently and is evidently still alive, but trapped. You turn to the maid who is standing on the shore and shout, 'They're still alive, I think they must all be alive.'

You scan along left and right and notice the occasional glint of gold. You drift left and then right from your original position and each time you come near to a bee you notice not one is dead, but merely trapped and wriggling relentlessly to escape their situation.

Digging your middle finger, thumb and index finger into the gravelly surface you pinch at each individual bee but cannot grip them firm. You try again and dislodge some of the small stones on the rock face.

Then you look down into your right palm and urge the bee with your mind to help you dig. It doesn't move. You want to call upon it, you need its help, but you do not know what to say. As you think tirelessly at ways you could help the stricken bees, the maid appears below you. You hover around six feet off the ground and she stares up at your dangling toes before shouting to you: 'Ah-Muzen-Cab. Address the bee in your hand as Muzen-Cab and it will help you.'

With this you look directly at the bee and its head appears to tilt back as though it was looking back at you. You begin to think hard about saving the bees in front of you and, as you reach out again with your left hand to start scraping, you notice the bee from your right hand fly up and start scurrying in a blurry golden light.

It digs in a whizzing, trembling action left and right of your own hand. It is as though a sparkler is scraping away at the stony rock face and before long you can see the bee which was trapped almost jump from its imprisoned state and fall into Muzen-Cab.

You then drift right to find another and then another and

soon the process becomes quicker and quicker the more specks of gold you find. You zoom around the island in a blur and as you do, the specks begin to merge and as you fly you notice a golden vapour trail following you at immense speed.

It is not long before you have circumnavigated the entire island and you do not want to stop. You look at the cliff face and with vigour you shout, 'Now rise!' The whole land mass before you drifts up from the scar line which the bees had made earlier. You implore the land to rise, 'More.' You scream again with a deep meaningful roar,

'More!' The island rises further still. You then soften your voice, 'Illuminate.' As beams of light discharge from your eyes, you light up the dark cavernous space before you and you fly inside.

You question yourself on how you are going to tip this huge land mass, this island, this country. What about your family, your friends...... what about civilization? A voice intrudes upon your daydream, 'Stop thinking.' You recognise the voice. It is not your own, but that of the maid who suddenly appears next to you, eyes bright white as she floats serenely.

'This has to be done, George. I can see your mind questioning your future actions. This must be done. The world needs to start again and you need to make it happen. This will be your toughest challenge, but once this island is turned we must hurry as there are hundreds, possibly thousands of land masses to turn.

'You are about to set a new equilibrium, a new existence and with this will come turmoil and destruction. The planet will start again, but you must begin the process now.'

As she says her last word the maid stops gliding next to you and hovers behind. You decide to continue moving forward and leave her in your wake. You slow to a halt and as you look back the maid appears as a white silhouette with her arms folded. She bellows through the darkness, 'Now!' Her command echoes all around you, loudly at first and then fading further and further away. You continue to move away from her and then stop. You speak to no-one but yourself. 'It must be here. We will lift here and this island will be plunged into the sea and that which is beneath the sea will rise and become land.'

As you scan around you notice a golden line in the distance. You turn back to find the maid. You explain to her, 'The bees have coordinated themselves.'

She replies, 'Under your command they will drive the land up and over. They will tip it into the sea.'

Without hesitating, you reply, 'Let us begin.'

You begin to will the land to move from above your head and as it starts to rise you lift your arms above your head and close your eyes. You will this ginormous land mass to rise further away from you. In what feels like minutes you continue to envisage the whole land mass of England, Wales and Scotland turn on its side into the Irish Sea. After several minutes, you sense a freshness to the air and open your eyes.

The sky is no longer dark and forlorn, it appears fresh and vibrant and blue. The sun hits your eyes. You can no longer look up. Just before you close your eyes to the blinding sun you make out the line of bees glittering like licks of flames. You urge them to continue pushing the island up and away. The maid tells you, 'This place is done.' And then she says,

'You must move on.'

You look at her and ask about the bees, 'But will they follow?'

Her response is clear, 'They belong to you.'

As you fall back to the shore the bright sun which blinded you from above comes tumbling towards you. You automatically cover your head and cower on the ground. You feel a thousand miniature prods all over your hunched back at the rear of your head. The maid mocks you, 'Get up. Show them you are their leader.'

The sun has not collapsed, it is the bees lighting the sky and like fragments of a space ship falling through the atmosphere they had appeared to be on fire, but you know this time you have to stay calm and let them come to you. You open your right palm and they start to land.

In your mind, you ask for speed and the flurry becomes like a wave. Soon you know it is time to leave these shores and move to another island, another land mass. The world was for turning.

Chapter 5

At first you follow the maid back into the depths of the sea where there are tube-like veins connecting the land masses. The complexity of these veins is mystifying, yet after three more islands you no longer follow the maid and start to lead the navigation amongst the tubes. Your speed of movement and navigation become faster and faster and before long you can see each tube glow gold with the vapour trail left in your wake.

As cities fall into the sea and people clamber to stay on their islands, countries lay in devastation turned completely on their side. Families torn apart, millions, if not billions of people perishing in the wreckage that ensues. Each land mass is tilted by you and the bees and yet you cannot see what is going on above. The maid sketches it out for you to help you

The cut of land mass and then the push upwards from the angle shown below will cause the land to tilt in this direction

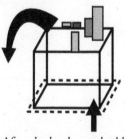

After the land mass had been cut it was elevated and tipped by George and the bees

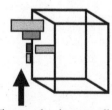

The new land mass will look like so after being tilted. The buildings will now be on their side

fully comprehend.

The buildings that once stood on the ground now exist only if their remnant foundations had been built strong enough. Most perish. The sheer weight of most buildings and the pull of gravity causes many to collapse. Many buildings situated in the wrong parts of their land become submerged under water and do not survive.

You look at the sketches made by the maid and understand what she meant by a 'new beginning'. The top surface of the land masses is now clear. Much of the land which once stood has been turned into the sea. As a consequence, marine life is decimated. The marine life which existed before the lands were turned is exposed to air for so long that most life perishes. The cataclysmic alterations to the world's environment has cost the lives of billions.

Was this right? Why did so many good people have to die? Questions whizz around your mind in a blur. The topography of the planet had been turned on its side, literally. There were now huge swathes of land that had been under water for millions of years, which now lay horizontal. New mountain ranges emerged and the rivers and channels which existed before now had new routes to the ocean. You imagine that only a handful of people have survived.

You reflect on what was before:- the buildings, the motorways, the cities, the forests and more importantly the people. Great Britain's population of around 70 million had been decimated. Larger land masses are turned including China, Russia, Kazakhstan, much of mainland Europe, India, Pakistan and the majority of the 'Middle East'. Billions of people have their lives turned upside down and only the luckiest, bravest and most courageous souls survive. The world will have to start again.

A new beginning

No buildings, no cars, but freedom and opportunity. You feel upset at the loss of life but exhilarated at the thought of starting something new. How could you bring about a worldwide society with fairness? Where a country's wealth and prosperity was not based on the exploitation of others. Taking their resources and using their people. No country now dominated another and where once there was wealth, now there was nothing. Where once there was poverty and famine, now there was nothing. The slate was clean.

A responsibility and a duty falls upon your shoulders to bring people together, unite all those who had survived and provide leadership to a more civilised and fairer society. You laugh at yourself and your own utopian ideals. You have already made assumptions that those who had survived needed a leader. That those who had survived wanted fairness and civility. People are different you think, some people will survive using their own ingenuity, whilst others will work together. Some people will seek advice and guidance, whilst others will tread their own path. Some people will share and help their neighbour, whilst others will steal and take from their neighbour.

The thought that the people may have survived buoys your sullen mood. Those people left in the world would have their own personalities, their own beliefs, their own background and ways of thinking. Just because the world has been turned on its side does not mean their personal views have to change. They will still act in a variety of ways and you have no right or control to alter their opinions.

New flora and fauna emerge from the darkest depths of the ocean as the land masses and islands of the world have been turned onto their side. Soon, this new life begins to flourish and spring up everywhere. Where once there was sea vegetation, new plants arise and begin to stretch upwards towards the sun.

The colours were bright and vibrant: you have never witnessed such pinks, yellows and turquoise flowers and navy-blue stems before. You marvel as this new vegetation starts to consume the barren land and then you notice insects, tiny and strange. Elongated tentacles at the front almost a metre in length, but fine like hair, and then their bodies appeared with several eyes down each side. You start to actively look for other life and find tortoise-like creatures with sharp fangs at the front of their beak. You notice the carcasses of sharks, whales and other sea life being eaten by an array of pink flies, crows, insects and these small tortoises which move quickly around in their armoured bodies.

As you wander amongst this new vegetation, the maid appears from behind a colossal, towering white reef. She says, 'This had been bleached from the rising sea temperatures and polluted waters.' The maid continues, 'Now all this wildlife has a new chance, a chance to bathe in sunlight, to be exposed to the elements, and what will emerge will be a new world, one in which you can lead.

You look at the maid as she hovers two feet above the

ground and reply, 'Err, yes, you keep referring to this leadership, but I cannot see anybody about and nor do I really want this responsibility, to be honest with you.

She looks you square in the eyes, 'It is not your choice. You are the one. Now run and keep running as you will never see me again. This is your time now, your time to make the Earth what you want it to be.'

With these final words the maid drifts away towards the thick vegetation that covered the land, beyond the vast mountain ridges and out of sight. You never see her again.

Chapter 6

You begin to run. You don't know where, but with the fresh wind against your face and the sense of adventure in your mind you just run. You go through lush green tropical plants, shrubs, algae-ridden rock formations and then begin to clamber a dark grey rock face. As you start to climb, bright pink birds fly out from their nest and startle you. Still you climb and soon you realise you are over 100ft in the air. As you look around at this new land you are amazed to see such a vast array of plants, shrubs and flowers.

The land lacks any large trees, but already you notice the odd seedling and know that soon there will be more vegetation. You reach the top of the rock you have been climbing and begin to run when you notice something rush across your path. You are hungry and wonder if this creature is something edible like a pig or a hog. You slowly follow the path of the creature and as quietly as possible you part the vegetation around you. Then you see it. It is standing stunned, stationary, only four feet in front of you. You notice its two rear paws with sharp claw-like nails and you can make out half a tortoise-like shell. The front of the animal is facing away from you and its head looks buried in the bushes in front of it.

You leap quickly onto the large tortoise shell back and immediately the rear legs of the creature start to kick back and scratch your chest and neck. You push down with your body weight and try to grapple with its head writhing left and right. You try and strangle the thing around its saggy neck, like a chicken. Eventually the creature's life is extinguished as it lies limp in your hold. You roll off from its shell and realise the creature had a beak and fang teeth at the front just like the ones you had seen eating carcasses of dead fish before. You feel guilty that one of the first things you have done in this new world is kill. Oddly your second thought is one of survival. You are a murderer and think to yourself, 'Am I some sort of psychopath?'

The sun is setting and you quickly realise you need a fire as it is getting cold all around. Gathering some kindling you try in desperation to remember the bush craft skills learnt from an adventure weekend your girlfriend had bought you in the old world. 'Yes!' you shout in delight, as a spark you have made from whacking two flint stones together has set off the kindling and you make fire.

You set up two pivots and stick a stake through the spine of the tortoise shell before roasting it and turning it slowly on your spit. It tastes delicious. Succulent and juicy and a flavour that is neither chicken, lamb or beef, but something new. A sweet flavour that you can not describe, but know you want more. After feeding, you close your eyes and begin a psychedelic journey into sleep.

The top of your skull feels as though it is melting into your brain and then your face begins to drip away from the edges of your jaw. Your eyes bulge out of your head as stars fall from the sky onto your exposed bony face, burning holes through the hard-white, bony, skeletal surface of your skull. In your slumber you rock your head from side to side to avoid the falling stars that are piercing these scorch holes in your face. The dream intensifies as maggots begin to climb up from the soil using the dripping skin that has fallen from your face in solidified droplets. As the maggots reach the top of this slippery, solidified gloop, like wax from a candle, they burrow into the holes made by the stars in your skull.

With this you feel your stomach contort and you wake up abruptly and projectile vomit into the burning embers of the fire you had made. You taste sick, it is repulsive, and it feels wet as it surges into the fire. As you sense the gush of the vomit, the wet slop against your head, you begin to realise you are in fact not a human anymore and have somehow, randomly become a tooth. Is it an effect of the poisonous turtle you had eaten or the new world you were in? Either way, a tongue licked over your face and you are sure, you are definitely now a tooth, but with conscious thought.

You look around and notice that everywhere is white. Fellow teeth surround you. You are, in fact, no longer part of your own face as you first thought; you are, in fact, a sharp, pointy fang. You notice another fang to your right; you have become the left fang of one of the tortoises you have just eaten.

This is no illusion, no hallucinogenic trip, you are now a single fang. You have no limbs, just visual and audio senses and a conscious mind. Soon you are munching on maggot infested whale meat. As you nose-dive into the rib cage of this decaying corpse you carve through the rotting flesh like a hot knife through butter. You feel sharp, you feel fresh and you feel like a fang.

This is so obscure, so surreal, but you can do nothing as

you go up and down in the mouth of a chelonioidea amniote. Every now and then a slimy wet goo slaps your back and covers you whole in saliva. After a while this blue slime becomes a welcome clean as you feel quite furry unless the thick pointy tongue of whatever creature's mouth you are in gives you a face slap. Although you feel trapped, you are weirdly relishing the experience of being a tooth. When you strike bone by accident, whilst gnawing on some flesh, it makes you wince with pain. Nerves run through you like shockwaves and you shudder for a split second or two. You have no control on where you go, nor what food your controller decides to consume, whenever they choose to do so.

One day you are being dragged along a dirty, dusty floor and grit bristles against your face as you begin to feel tiny, tiny paws start to climb over your face. You immediately think you may be nose deep in something like an ant's nest or termite mound and before long you are severing heads, tearing bodies in two and on some occasions popping what feel like mini air capsules. You assume the mini air capsules to be either the heads of the insects popping or the stomachs of the insects bursting.

As time passes you begin to get a severe head ache as if part of your skull has been removed. You can't shake it and try to reason why this would be. Then it dawns on you that you had bit down on a hard surface two days earlier and you had been chipped. Soon your pain starts to permeate through your whole being. You feel sick. It hurts to pierce food and soon you notice the creature whose mouth you were in is moving more slowly and is in pain too. You stop eating meat and on occasion strip leaves of a bush, but you are dying and you know it. One day, feeling lifeless and devoid of energy, you fall from the mouth of the creature carrying you in its jaws. Face down in the dirt you feel the air compressing around you as you are stamped on into the mud. Buried beneath a bush you close your eyes. The next time you will experience anything will be months from now.

Over time your bony body separates into tiny microscopic miniscule fragments, but why can you still feel this? Why is there a sense of your broken parts? Surely, if as a human you lost a limb, you would not sense these separated parts? You begin to feel a huge suction and force taking you upwards from the soil you lay in.

The fragments of your bony tooth swirl violently around as you are whisked up into a light green tube. You are inside the xylem tissue of a plant and you get transported to a leaf. Soon you feel your body expand and the bony parts that once were became malleable, soft and green. Whenever the sun shines on you it feels amazing; your skin tingles, you feel a surge of energy and your body expands. As you grow the sensations of this warm glow are matched only by the refreshing quench of thirst which comes from the rainwaters. You are a leaf.

As a leaf you experience a new existence, one filled with the sensual touch of insects such as butterflies and orchrilipeads. The orchrillipeads are a new species of insect which have survived the turning of the oceans and the formations of the new lands. These insects have slug- like underbellies and huge, long tentacles at the front of their stick-like eyes. They survive through eating the mini larvae of flies but seem to work in unison with the plant you are attached to. Cleaning the leaves and making you feel fresh every time they shimmy across your surface.

For the first time in a long time you begin to think about the seasons and you assume it is summer due to the hot days and the tightening of your skin. Soon, though, the insects stop coming and winds begin to move you; you feel cold and the water that rushes through your veins now trickles and seeps into you. You feel the edges of your face wrinkle and tighten; the bright green colour that you once were begins to fade. You wither and feel weak, weary and sense the end is near. You begin to glide to the floor and this is the first time you feel detached and devoid of life. You lay there face down in the boggy mud; insects begin to devour you and larger creatures tread over the top of you.

It is a miserable end, you feel torn apart. Like the disintegration of the tooth you feel bereft of life. You die and become mushy, slushy bog-like mud. Moist and full of nutrients from soil and water life suddenly begins to spring from your body. You feel roots spread through you like veins and shoots start to grow vertically towards the sky. As the seasons change you harden and begin to crack. Winds take away your top surface and your skin begins to burn. You are mud, you are the earth of the world.

Insects crawl on you and inside of you but you feel nothing. As summer passes and autumn comes around clouds start to fill with rain and day after day you begin to loosen and soften with every rain drop. Before long, as autumn turns to winter, you become submerged; no longer exposed to the sky, you fall under several centimetres of water. As sediment, you break up and drift in the water. You take on this liquid form and feel free. Flowing around the branches of trees, swirling between rocks and crashing down the side of a mountain you are exhilarated at this liberty. Never have you felt this energised as you flow towards the new seas of the world. You feel fresh, free and full of energy as all around you are tiny specks of life. Plankton are everywhere and you know this is a sign that larger marine life must exist in the oceans. You are water.

As winter sets in the temperature drops; you are far away from land at sea. You are part of the vast ocean and drift with the currents that sweep around the earth. The first creatures of size you come across are small, silvery and agile. They glint in the midday sun and swim as large schools forming huge shadows around you. You are surrounded by sardines. As they rush around, you envy their camaraderie; they appear to be having fun, to be working together and sharing in one another's company. You decide to join them. You become a fish, a sardine.

Swimming as part of a pack feels great: you intertwine with one another, dodging and weaving and following the crowd. Together you seem invincible, a swarm of power as you twirl through the oceans. You buzz past rocky shorelines, dive into the depths and dance with the sparkles of the sun on the surface. One day, as you play with your friends, you notice an ominous black shadow looming above and a sense of fear reverberates throughout the school. You all begin to swim downwards, but you feel an enormous sucking force drag you to the surface and inside a dark eery vacuous hole.

You slip down a slimey tract and then feel your skin begin to burn. Looking around at the other sardines they are squealing and wriggling in pain as they dissolve in the acidic liquid you now find yourself in. Without a second thought, you begin to swim as hard as you can towards the slimey tract that was at least two feet above and away from your head. You wriggle and splash and then try your hardest to leap, but to no avail. Exhausted you begin to slide deeper and deeper down and your skin melts and burns. You dissolve.

When you open your eyes, you feel a surge of power come from your Brobdingnagian tail. You are immense, a huge body of muscle gliding through the ocean at will with a sense of ownership and bravado. You immediately realise you are a king amongst the little fish which swim around you. They appear in your vision as minute white specks in the sun as you swim near the surface of the sea. Most of your time is spent much deeper in the dark depths of the ocean where you would idly roll in the algid sea just to entertain yourself. On occasion, you follow a pod of dolphins but as they catch sight of you they immediately turn away and swim in an opposite direction.

At times you are omnipotent, but soon you found yourself to be quite lonely, swimming around with no friends, no purpose. You become bored and drift with the currents of the sea. You ponder what you could do to add some excitement to your life and although eating is a tasty distraction to your boredom it soon becomes obvious you need a partner.

This becomes your goal and you swim for miles and miles

in the vague hope of finding a female bryde whale. You have almost lost hope and begin to feel sorry for yourself when a beautiful giant emerges from the depths. You follow her for months, circling her and trying to catch her attention with your enormous tale and spectacular ability to encircle large schools of fish to consume. Soon your persistence pays dividends and after mating and a long period of gesticulation your partner give birth to a son. You feel overwhelmed, but know this emotional journey is soon to end as intuitively a dark cloud hung in your tiny brain. Your capture is imminent.

A searing pain in your back causes an almighty spasm through your spine and makes you thrash around in agony. As each giant spear pierces your thick skin the excruciating torture drives you lower. You find the pain interminable as you try to swim away from whoever has attacked you. In your distress the lower you swim the sharper the pain becomes. You are unaware that you had been pierced by several spears with long taut wreaths attached to them.

These basic, javelin-type instruments of death have been crudely constructed by hunters who have survived the turning of the lands. They have sharpened remnant pieces of metal to fashion spear heads attached to long wooden spears and vine wreaths. As the hunters yank and heave on the spears, you are pulled nearer to the surface and your fate is sealed as more and more spears impale your thick grey skin to reveal copious amounts of blood. The sea turns red around you as you swim slower and slower until all life has drained away from your body and you become limp. Your last memories are being dragged onto a boat before the exhaustion and pain consumes your body. Then darkness.

Chapter 7

Y ou sit around a fire happy with the fish you have caught that day. Two days have passed since you arrived to meet a group of people who had just caught an almighty whale. You begin to think what it would be like to be a whale or even a fish, a bird, a tree or even the land you walked upon as a human, but your memory is short.

The only thing that occupies your mind each day is surviving. The world has been turned on its side, but you have no knowledge of this at first, only discovering this strange truth when talking to the others around the campfire. The only memories you have are those from the two days you have been with the people around the campfire; you cannot recall the past. It strikes you, listening to the group talk, that not once have you seen another person die, nor a building fall, nor encountered the disaster they had all been discussing.

You do not know what has happened, you have only heard through those you are with now; you have to trust their word. You just feel lucky to be alive.

The world has been turned on its side and although you try desperately to remember what has happened, you can not recall a thing. You have to rely completely on the stories of the people who you had stumbled upon. James, Mick, Hayley, Bob and Tracy.

James had been an international banker for most of his life. Spending much of his time jetting between New York,

London and Tokyo and rarely seeing his family. The millions he had made were of no interest to him, for James it was all about the sell. He loved to negotiate, he loved to get the best deal and business came first. In his prime, James owned the highest penthouses of New York, London and Tokyo; he mixed with finance ministers, corporate giants and hedge fund executives. James liked to jog, but his mistress preferred him to stay in bed. He could only see her on Sundays whilst his wife Penelope took the children to church. This previous existence, this previous life, this was dead. James was now a hunter, constantly scouring the land and seas for food to survive each day.

Mick used to be an HGV (heavy goods vehicle) driver. Mick regaled you with stories of his cab, over 100 DVDs, his own bed behind the passenger seat, 7 cups of tea a day and over 5000 miles a week across Europe.

Mick has coffee stained teeth and a hot temper, often losing his composure when trying to start a fire at night. Mick is Latvian and is philosophical about this new world. His view is that 'we're in it together now and we might as well get on with it'. Mick has never married but did have a brother who had moved to Germany and a sister who was studying in Leeds, England. In one of your first nights talking to Mick he sadly said: 'I guess those places don't exist anymore. Still, might as well get on with it, we're in this together.' Mick often repeats his own phrases, but he has a heart of gold and is willing to help anyone.

Tracy had been a cleaner and a mother to four little girls. Tracy cries most days, but her suffering is hidden by her beautiful smile and cackling laughter when the group chat in the evenings. It is obvious in Tracy's bright blue eyes that she is in constant anguish at the loss of her family. She tries desperately to help the group each day in whatever way she can, whether this be hunting, gathering, cleaning, preparing, or cooking. In her own way, Tracy is a leader as she is always willing to muck in for the good of the group. Tracy has a warm character: she is caring, considerate and always willing to listen to others. Her diminutive stature at just four feet and ten inches with curly blond hair and compassionate demeanour endears her to everyone in the group.

Bob is the complete opposite of Tracy. An aggressive old man with grey wispy hair, ginger stubbly beard and a fake gold tooth which glinted in the midday sun. He regularly eulogises about leading a group of financial advisers to their best ever sale figures before the cataclysmic events that turned everyone's world upside down.

Bob thinks he knows the answer to everything; he thinks he is the world's leading expert in everything. When, in actual fact, he just wants to be liked. Before he trained as a financial adviser, Bob had labouring jobs, first of all as a deck hand on a boat and then as a storeman in a warehouse. Although old he is strong and able to build rafts to help the group go fishing and build implements for us to go hunting.

Hayley had been a teacher. She is athletic, slightly anxious, but always willing to lend a hand. Sometimes Hayley would be seen sitting alone and crying for her lost son and her mother who she misses dearly. An efficacious character, Hayley works hard for the group and had befriended Tracy as the only other woman.

They are often heard gossiping to each other long into the

night. Never malicious, they speak only of their lost families and for the future survival of those they now found themselves with. Hayley is a pretty girl with a svelte figure, blond hair and toned legs who many of the men lust after, but to whom she shows little interest.

That is the group. Six in total, lost in a new world, but together trying to make sense of it all and start again. Your own journey to this point was a blur and so you had limited stories to share with the group about your previous life. This lack of certainty puts Bob on edge and he asks you one evening in a very forthright manner: 'So where did you come from again?

You have to think on the spot and give a spurious reply, 'I think near Tracy actually, err yeah, near London, well actually just outside.'

Bob retorted: 'No, no. I don't mean where in the world you came from. The other night you seemed to appear out of the fire when we were cooking the whale we had just caught during the day.'

You look puzzled and you reply hesitantly, mumbling: 'Oh… I was errr… walking… and… err… just stumbled across your fire at night… you know in the dark, it sort of attracted me.'

You pause as you are unclear yourself as to what had actually happened. You hope your story will wash with Bob who looks very suspicious. You had, in fact, morphed into a human after only hours previously been swimming in the oceans as a whale. Unfortunately, you have no recollection of this due to the inordinate amount of pain inflicted upon you when you had been hunted.

They had completely numbed your senses with their handmade spears and in turn anaesthetised your mind. You had blocked out the pain and your mind could not recall what you used to be. So, all you can say to further elaborate on your own back story is: 'I have been on my own for months searching for other life and scouring the land to find someone, to find anything. When I saw the smoke from your fire I came running towards your campsite and by the time I had got here the sun had set and it was dark. Fortunately, I could still smell the fire through the forest and must have entered your campsite from behind the bushes.'

Bob's suspicion seems to subside as he begins to nod and look a little more sympathetic to what you are saying. However, his reply to you is somewhat different to the impression you are getting from his body language. Bob questions you, 'Oh, right, so did you steal some of our catch too?'

Tracy angrily responds to his suggestion, 'Whoa hold up there Bob, that's bang out of order. This man has only just turned up here, we don't know his name or anything about him and you're already accusing him of stealing our food.'

Bob is evidently annoyed, 'Well you can't blame me Trace. That whale was massive and when he turned up from nowhere, standing by our fire, our huge catch seemed to disappear. We were left with him standing in exactly the same place where the whale had been lying, next to the fire!'

You need to reassure this guy: 'Look, I certainly didn't steal your catch and I have no idea where your whale meat has gone. All I can tell you is I saw the smoke, headed towards your camp and here I am.'

Tracy is quick to lend her support, 'No trouble darling, he's a bit tetchy when it comes to his grub, our Bob.'

Hayley then shouted over from the back of the camp, 'Yeah, don't worry about moody pants. Anyway, you should be a veggie like me, Bob, then you wouldn't be so angry all the time!' Hayley starts to laugh to herself and you can see Bob's face start to smile. 'I'm sorry lad, it's just so sad. That day we caught the whale we thought we were going to feast for days. Then you arrived and the whale meat...... well, it just disappeared. I hope you can see where I'm coming from?'

You nod to show your respect. You can understand the solemn mood of the camp. Bob looks up from the floor: 'Anyway what's your name lad, it's good to build our little colony.'

You snigger a little at his lame joke and then weirdly and without consciously thinking you spurt out, 'George.'

You see a tall black man come towards the fire from near where Hayley was stood at the back of the fire. James looks over to you across the fire and says, 'A true Englishman's name, if ever I did hear.' James has long gangly legs and strides into the campsite with his thin frame and elongated stride. He outstretches his hand to shake yours and speaks eloquently, 'Hello, I'm James and I'm pleased we appear to finally have some-one in the camp with a bit of class.'

The others laugh as James looks down at them with disdain from his seven feet tall frame. You aren't sure if he is being serious, but by the laughter of the others you think the whole situation is a bit 'tongue in cheek'. So, you reply in kind, 'I aim to please.' James languidly bends down with a wry smile on his face exaggerated by the fire burning beside him.

As he prods at the flames with a stick he embarks on a

philosophical tirade about the reasons why we are all here. James' primary argument is that God had chosen certain people to survive just as in the case of Noah and the Ark. James' belief is the mixed backgrounds and skills of the group had proven to him that God had ensured there was the right mix of males, females, races, mental and physical capabilities and togetherness to survive and start over.

The group is starting to lose interest in James' diatribe and Tracy intervenes: 'But James…' She pauses and then says, 'No-one cares what you think!' The whole group roar with laughter and James drops his stick into the fire. As everyone else rolls around laughing you watch him throw his arms up in the air with despair. Hayley adds another insult in his direction as he starts to walk away from the campfire: 'Yeah and you're not getting in my knickers either!'

The whole group continue to howl with laughter. Sullen, James is already walking off to the edge of the camp where he finds a small cove and you watch as he beds down for the night. It makes you think, are you really the only six people left on the planet after it had been turned on its side?

That night you sit around the fire and listen to the others tell of how they had come across one another and then became united as a group. They all seem united in both their individual grief for lost ones, but in their determination to make the best out of their current situation. Mick has electrical engineering knowledge and is desperate to come across some power source to help the group generate power or, even better, create some sort of electrical current. They try each day to scour the land and dig in the rubble to find what they can.

Bob is a jack of all trades and helps lift, carry, build and cook. He is keen to help Mick but has a rather pessimistic outlook on the likelihood of the group ever trying to generate their own electricity. The two ladies, Tracy and Hayley, both come from England. Tracy lived in the Midlands, Barrow-upon-Soar to be precise, between Leicester and Loughborough, whilst Hayley is from Romford in Essex. James is from Nigeria and had moved to America when he was eleven.

His tall, slender frame makes James appear relaxed as he moves around the campsite, but his mind is razor sharp and he is well respected by the group for presenting some of the best ideas for their survival.

In the morning you set off with James leading you all into the undergrowth. The floor is thick with sludge and as you wade through you can hear the slip slop of those following behind. You venture forwards for what feels like hours and soon Tracy and Hayley start to moan: 'How much further.... I'm starving.... Where are we going?'

The midday sun is searing through the long palmate leaves that hang overhead. Every now and then the flickering light finds a gap in the forest and burns the ferric rich iron soil. This reminds you of Kenya where you have been once before on holiday. Then you realise, a memory had emerged, a distant memory. You long for more and pray that different experiences may spark a lightbulb in your mind.

Right now, you have no idea geographically where you were in the old world so your mind drifts to the time you were in Iten, in the Kenyan Rift Valley, marvelling at the iron rich red soil that surrounded you. Mick, whose full name is

Mikelis, and Bob, who is actually Robert from Australia, are walking together and can see you daydreaming and start to laugh hysterically in your direction. You take offense at their laughter and ask: 'What? What are you two laughing at?'

James looks back and he too smiles broadly and points to your head. As you place your hand on your scalp you feel a gooey, bitty substance and you immediately think something has defecated on you from above.

What is strange is that you can see no birds above, nor monkeys or creatures in the trees. As you continue to look around the overhanging leaves you see some slimy gel-type substance drop from the point of a leaf.

You look at the floor and notice the red soil steaming where it has fallen and turned a turquoise blue. You immediately shout to the group: 'Stop, stop. Come and have a look at this.' As the group gather around the gooey steaming mess on the floor you explain what you have just seen and Bob then throws out an open question to the group: 'I wonder what it is? Does anyone know what substances are in it to make the soil turn blue like that?'

You all continue to stare and Tracy starts to talk, 'Is it me, or are there speckly, shiny bits in that goo?'

Hayley agrees, 'Yeah, yeah, I can see them too. It reminds me of that edible, gold paper they put on posh food when you watch those cooking shows.'

James bends down on one knee and slowly takes out what appears to be a monocle from his pocket. It is obviously some sort of microscope and he stares longingly at the goo for what seems like an age.

Mick cannot take the delay and asks, 'Well?'

James looks up at him, 'They're moving.'

Mick appears confused and bends down towards James, 'What's moving?'

Everyone now starts to look at the goo on the floor and from afar it just represents a vibrant blue splodge surrounded by the red soil. But then you hear the excitement in Mick's gruff East European accent: 'The gold specks, you seem them. Look, they're alive. They're like little tadpoles, but smaller, all swimming around and when they hit each other they sparkle. It's amazing, come and have a look.'

You kneel down with the others all surrounding the blue gloop on the floor whilst James' monocle magnifying glass is passed around. To all of your amazement these tiny creatures are generating what appears to be small flashes of light when they hit each other. You have an idea. 'James, put me on your shoulders, I've got an idea.'

As you reach up to an overhanging leaf you scrape off a layer of this thick mucus-type substance onto the floor.

James lowers you to the floor and you beckon the others to gather round this small puddle. You try to push the liquid gunk together, closer and thicker, and as you do so the flashes appear brighter as more of these minuscule creatures crash into one another. Mick is mesmerised: 'Surely, if we collect a load of this stuff and try and contain it in a small area, some container of some sort, then at night we would have a constant glow or light.'

Bob agrees, 'That's a great idea. We just need to find some sort of container, or to think of something we could make ourselves'

Hayley replies, 'I know something we could do. When we

were walking through the forest there were some white flowers; if the petals are strong enough we could join them together somehow and pour the goo in. The white would let the light shine through.

Tracy scoffs, 'How are you going to join petals together? We need something stronger as petals will just wilt when this stuff goes inside them.'

Hayley is not impressed with Tracy's riposte, 'OK, so what's your recommendation, clever clogs?'

Hayley stands still and looks at Tracy with her arms folded. Tracy takes a couple of seconds and then replies, 'I'm not sure yet, we need to keep searching for something that's transparent, strong and watertight.' Tracy is struggling to think of anything on the spot and Hayley is quick to jump on her hesitancy and lack of imagination, 'Oh, that's right, repeat what's already been said. It's not that easy is it!'

Hayley is rolling her eyes in contempt. James tries to quell the bickering pair. 'Come on you two, let's carry on along the path and we might come across something.'

Bob then raises his arm all of a sudden, to garner the attention of the group, 'Hold on a minute, shouldn't we at least mark this point as we know this substance is here.'

James acknowledges Bob's idea, 'Yeah, nice one, Bob, that's a great thought.'

Bob and Mick tear down several branches and you help them pile up a big mound of leaves on the red trail to act as a marker.

As you set off together you trek through overgrown plants and fallen trees for around 15 minutes before coming across some sort of concrete outline of a small building jutting out from the soil. It looks like the old concrete gun huts from the Second World War which sporadically occupied the odd field in Northern France and Southern England.

As you get nearer you see a large concrete frame similar in size to a football goal but tilted at a peculiar angle. The left-hand post is protruding around three feet out of the floor, whilst the right-hand post protrudes around six feet out of the floor with a long, diagonal, concrete cross beam connecting the angled vertical posts. The width of each post and beam is the same at around thirty centimetres and as you peer inside the lopsided 'goal mouth' of the building was nothing but black darkness, not even a sound.

Immediately your inquisitive nature wants to go in and explore and Bob can see you thinking. 'You want to go in there, don't you?'

You reply, 'Well yes, of course, we've been trekking for hours and found nothing and you guys have been together for how long and never found anything, so let's have a look.'

Bob is quick to quash your assumption, 'Er, you're wrong in your assumption there, son. Before you come along we found each other and individually we have seen all sorts, but we don't take unconsidered risks and that's why we are all still here. We're alive because we don't take unnecessary risks.'

You let out a primal scream in exasperation at your perceived lack of support from Bob. The sheer fact he has repeated himself when talking annoys you. Let alone his negative sentiment. Mick comes jogging over from the back of the group, as everybody looks on in silence.

'Whoa, whoa, whoa! Can everyone calm down, it's hot, we're all tired and I think it's a good idea if we just chill out for a bit and then make a decision as a group.'

Mick defuses the situation and the girls who are trying to look at the floor to avoid the altercation gather with James, you and Bob.'

Hayley slumps to the floor, whilst Tracy has a little peak inside the concrete frame before sitting next to her friend. Tracy looks up from her seated position, 'I am soooooooo thirsty. Has anyone got any water?' Unbeknown to you James has been carrying two bottles of fresh water for the whole trek. It makes you realise that James is both organised and has everyone's best interests at heart. As the water is passed around you ask:

'Where did you get this from James?'

James replies, 'I went on one of those corporate survival weekends and they show you how to survive off the land. There are seven signs to an ancient, old, growth forest and one of them is running drinking water.' James pauses and starts to look around into the dense forest surrounding us. 'We learnt how to navigate to the water, filter it and use it to survive.'

Whilst listening to James it dawns on you that this man is keeping the group alive through his knowledge of bushcraft and survival skills. You want James' opinion on heading into the black abyss beyond the concrete doorway. 'What do you think, James?'

James, in his usual relaxed style, looks at the group longingly, 'What have we got to lose?'

Before Bob can destroy James' adventurous spirit, James quickly continues, 'I know, I know Bob, I can see what you are thinking and you're probably right. We've come this far surviving on our instincts and our teamwork but, Bob, that's all we're doing, surviving.'

James looks each of us in the eye and exposes his inner feelings: 'To be honest, I've had enough. Day after day we search in vain, for what? For scraps of food that will keep us alive until we find some more food, but for what? Why are we surviving? What sort of existence is this anyhow? I'm bored. I'm bored of hunting, I'm bored of being cold, I'm bored of telling you guys what you can and cannot eat from the ground and the sea. I NEED something more. This is not living – this ain't no life for me.'

James then slumps onto the smaller of the two concrete posts and puts his head between his knees. Tracy and Hayley shuffle over to comfort him whilst Mick and Bob look around themselves in a bewildered state unable to fixate on anything.

James looks up from the floor: 'Look, when we were walking through the undergrowth, I saw some giant, translucent, umber mushrooms. If they're strong enough we could turn them upside down, hold them by their stalk and fill their translucent cups with the goo. Surely then we would have some sort of glow when we entered this darkness. We've just got to hope the stalks are strong enough'

He gestures with his thumb pointing over his shoulder into the black abyss behind him. You are quick to lend support: 'Well I'm in.' Bob grunts back at you, 'We already know that.'

Bob then looks down at James and says, 'Listen, mate, you're the reason I'm still alive now so I'm with you, buddy, whatever you say, Captain.'

You look at Mick: 'And you?'

Mick retorts rhetorically, 'Well I'm not staying out here on my own, am I?'

As you look down towards the girls who both still have their arms round James, they look up at you and nod in unison. Buoyed by the unanimous backing of the group you say, 'Right then, you three stay here and Mick, Bob, let's go fill some mushrooms!'

Before setting back into the undergrowth you ask James where exactly these giant mushrooms are. After listening intently to the instructions of James, you set off back into the great unknown along with Mick and Bob. The three of you walk at pace as you want to get back before dark sets in. As you briskly walk along you turn to Mick and Bob and ask, 'How are you guys for jogging?'

Bob pours scorn on your suggestion: 'Look, young whipper snapper. You've got us coming back, but don't push your luck.'

You realise Bob is right, "OK, OK. I was just asking.'

Mick laughs as Bob grumbles under his breath. You make your way back along the route from which you have come, and, in the distance, you make out the pile of leaves you had laid down before, as a marking point for the sticky, gooey-like substance.

After spotting the leaves you exclaim, 'Look, you guys, wait here whilst I jog on and go find these giant mushrooms James was on about.'

Mick looks at you with a deep, meaningful glare and says, 'Do you really think it is a good idea to be going into the undergrowth on your own?'

You are confident: 'It's OK, James said he saw them not too far away when we were walking along, I'm sure I'll be fine. I'll be back in two minutes.'

You begin to walk back along the well-trodden track you had followed and remember what James had said. He clearly said to look for the tree with pink flowers and large dark green overhanging leaves and you will see the mushrooms close to the base of the tree.

You walk further and further down the path, but you can not find the tree. You then thought it would be easier to come back towards Mick and Bob and to look left and right as this was the way James would have been looking when you had all walked down the same path earlier. You start to walk back and assiduously stare at every tree you walk past. Then it hits you, bright vibrant pink flowers with long dark overhanging leaves.

As you step off the track into the thick undergrowth you feel your feet start to sink in the soil. They are sinking quickly so you try desperately to move away from the sodden soil, but your feet do not budge. In a moment of panic, you quickly scream for help. You stand there unable to move as you slide deeper and deeper into the soil. 'Help!' You scream louder: 'Heeelllllppp!!!'

You are now up to your waist and look all around you to see if there is anything you can grab to pull yourself free, when you notice the mushrooms. They almost glow and lure you towards their delicate luminosity, but you cannot reach them and at that moment you begin to sink further and further.

The soil has now consumed over three quarters of your

body and is now up to your chest, when Bob turns up looking for you. He is just about to open his mouth before you say, 'OK, Bob, I admit it, you were right. Now, just get me out of here.' Bob grabs your arms and pushes his feet against the tree to help get more leverage. Gradually, you feel the slimy soil start to come away from your chest. 'Keep going, Bob, we're almost there.' Bob's face is bright red by now as he pulls both your arms with all his might. Soon, you can feel your waist lift out of the mud and you try desperately to wriggle your legs to help Bob.

It is no luck; Bob is exhausted and you can see he is drained. As he rests momentarily you sink a couple of inches back into the wet soil. You try to encourage Bob out of sheer desperation: 'Don't stop, Bob, I'm slipping back in.' As you look at his face Bob is drenched in sweat and his face is purple red like a beetroot. You plead, 'Please Bob.' You whimper desperately, 'Just one last big effort.'

He heaves with everything he has and as the soil passes your thighs you know you are going to be free. Bob collapses under the tree, spread-eagled with his legs on the path. Your head laid next to his ankles. As you peer up towards Bob, his head is propped up against a tree and he looks back at you and says, 'I told you not to come alone.' You both laugh out loud for quite a while. After the laughter stops, you cry without Bob seeing, as you know you have been close to death. You try to snap out of it and summon Bob: 'Right then, let's grab what we came here for and get back to Mick.'

As you climb up to Bob he is staring longingly at the mushrooms. He turns to you and says, 'They're beautiful, aren't they?'

You look at them and nod hypnotically, 'Yep, they sure are.'

Bob looks concerned. 'Seems a shame to tear them out of the soil.' Although you can see Bob's point of view, you have to reassure him: 'I know, I know, but we've got to do it Bob, that's the reason we came back. Come on.'

After a little bit of cajoling you and Bob start to tug at the base of the giant translucent mushrooms. Bob is clearly tired from his previous exertions so it is left to you to do most of the yanking.

After uprooting two of the behemoths, you look at Bob, 'How many do you think we need?'

Bob looks around the forest floor. 'Well there's only one really big one left, let's take that last one and be done with it.'

As you heave and toil to get the last mushroom out of the ground the tree you are under starts to creak. Bob is leaning against it and he starts to shake and tremble as though he is being shaken by a pneumatic drill. 'The bloody tree's vibrating. Quick, let's get out of here.'

As you quickly scamper up the path the tree begins to fall towards you and Bob. You frantically shout at him, 'Quick, run!'

The tree crashes inches from Bob's head. You immediately joke with him: 'See, I knew I'd get you to run eventually.'

Bob is quick to defend himself: 'Well I knew this little trip back was a bad idea. Now let's get back to Mick and get out of here.'

The translucent mushrooms are much heavier than you expected, and they slow your progress back towards Mikelis. As you trek back along the path you had followed you begin to marvel at the different shades of green reflected off the leaves around you.

Some parakeets fly out from a tree overhead and their bright green feathers are camouflaged against the foliage around them. Juniper green, sage green, fern green, olive green, chartreuse and pine green all blended together in a wave of vegetation which vacillates in the strong breeze now blowing in your face. The branches on the trees around begin to dance up and down as you hurry back to Mick. You think he might be getting cold.

Soon you see the muscly Latvian stood in amazement staring at the floor. As you follow his gaze you can see thousands of little sparks bouncing around off the floor. He turns to the two of you and says, 'I thought I'd be constructive and get as much of this glutinous stuff off the leaves as I could.'

You are impressed with Mick's initiative, 'Good thinking, pal.'

Bob looks at you both with wearisome eyes and says begrudgingly, 'We now need to scoop it into these things. They already weigh a tonne, so God knows what they're going to be like filled up with that stuff.'

You try to inject some energy into the situation: 'Right guys, no time to waste. Just shovel it in with your hands and let's hope for the best.'

You and Bob lay the mushrooms on the floor and the three of you begin to scoop the thick viscous goo into the giant translucent cups. The enclosed mushroom cups begin to sparkle gold and as you look across to Bob and Mikelis they have big gleaming smiles plastered across their faces.

The sun is beginning to drop in the sky and so you toil back with the heavy mushrooms along the muddy path. As you arrive back to Tracy, James and Hayley they are all asleep on the floor. Bob decides to shout at them in a sarcastic tone: 'Oi, you lot! Wakey, wakey, it looks like you've been busy.'

Tracey is having none of Bob's cynicism: 'Well we've got some wood to start. All you have done is go for a walk.'

Bob rolls his eyes and looks at you with a knowing expression: 'Yes, you could say that.'

Hayley picks up on his inference, 'Why, what happened?'

You sit down next to the three of them: 'Let's get a fire started and we'll tell you all about it.'

Chapter 8

You awake to the glowing embers of a fire. It is dusk and the sun is starting to rise. You had laughed long into the night and your throat is sore and your mouth is dry. You lean over James' prone body to see if his canisters have any water left in them. A tiny amount is left, and it is enough to wet your mouth. Your rustling seems to disturb Hayley who is asleep next to the concrete post of the doorway you had gathered around. She gestures towards the canister you have just drank from and you show her it is empty by tipping it upside down and shaking.

Gradually the whole group starts to awaken from their slumber and it is soon clear that the whole group is thirsty for water. James speaks first and says what you were all thinking: 'Before we go in there, we must find water.'

Everyone nods, but then silence falls across the group as no-one knows where to go to find water. James throws his arms up into the air and looks at you: 'See what I mean; it always falls on me.' James stomps off past where you had camped into a new section of the forest.

'Wait, wait,' you shout after him as you jog to catch up. The others stay behind as you catch-up with James. You say, 'Look, I understand how much pressure you must feel being constantly relied upon. I'm here to help you. I haven't got your bushcraft skills, but I am willing to help in any way I can.'

James does not respond to you and keeps walking for a bit.

He looks in a contemplative mood before he starts to talk in front of himself rather than turning to face you. As he carries on walking, he says, 'It's nothing personal. Just like I said the other night, I'm fed up. It's always me. I'm keeping them alive and I've had enough of the responsibility. Look over there.'

As you look forward towards where James is pointing there seems to be some sort of water spray mist. You carry on to a parting in the trees and are met with a sheer drop, hundreds of feet below. Looking across this huge chasm to another sheer rock face across from you is a huge waterfall tumbling down into a deep ravine at the bottom of the two cliffs. You turn to James: 'I didn't realise we were so high up.' He is as surprised as you. 'Nope, neither did I. It looks as though we need to get down there if we want any water.'

You sit on the edge together, dangling you legs over the three hundred feet drop to the bottom of ravine. Both of you marvelling at the beauty of the huge waterfall in front of you as it sparkles, fizzes and effervesces with its immense natural beauty.

It dawns on you that James is similarly fearless to you and with his leadership James has kept the group alive and motivated for several months. You want to harness James' influence on the group as you know the only way to move forward is to work together. You speak in the direction of the waterfall: 'Do you think that the concrete doorway could lead down there, to the bottom of that waterfall?'

James appears dismissive: 'What, you think someone had dug a 300ft tunnel from the surface to the river?'

You are quizzical: 'How else are we going to get down there?'

James sits there for a while thinking about your question and he gets up and walks back around 30 metres looking all around him. The forest is dense and you can sense he is trying to think of a way to make it down. As he looks around, you wonder if he is going to come back to you with a route to make it through the forest and down to the water. For a split second you think he has reneged on venturing into the dark abyss and is conjuring an alternate plan. Then James eventually breaks his silence: 'Right. I've got an idea. I'll give you two options and you can make the final decision.' James is speaking at you whilst walking back towards the cliff edge where you were sat looking at him. You reply, 'Go on, I'm listening.' As he gets closer to you, James suddenly veers off into the forest and starts shouting: 'I'll be back in two minutes. Don't move.'

You sit patiently worried about James going into an area you know is dangerous after almost losing your own life only a day earlier. Soon, as promised, you hear rustling come through the trees and James emerges with his arms dragging something behind him.

James' biceps and deltoids are bulging with veins popping out of his muscular arms. He is dripping with sweat and perspiration fell from his brow and runs down his face and across his swollen arm muscles. He is dragging vines which are thick like the ropes big boats use to tie themselves to port. These natural vines look heavy, look long and look sturdy. Proudly, James proclaims: 'I present to you, liana.' James drops the vines on the floor.

'Whose Liana?' you ask, wondering if James had stumbled across some indigenous tribal woman in the forest. He rolls his eyes at your lack of knowledge.

'Liana is the long vine type stems I have dragged what felt like miles to show you. These natural thick ropes will help us climb. Remember Tarzan swinging from tree to tree? Well, this is the natural sort of rope type vine he would have used. So, I'm giving you choices, Georgey boy. Do you want to abseil down this cliff edge with the others or shall we bang in some stakes at the top of the gateway, wrap some vine around them and our waists and venture in. You know that we can have at least some security both to know our way out if we lose luminosity and if we fall down any crevasses inside that dark hole.'

You look at the coiled liana on the floor and are immediately impressed by the way they look and then, after touching, by the way the felt. They appear to have some sort of natural strength to them and yet they are malleable enough for you to shape if you put some muscle behind bending them.

'Look, there's no way I'm going to try convincing Bob to abseil down that.' You point down the huge ravine. 'I think it best that we drag these two vines back to the others and tell them we're going in. Let's explain the situation, see if we can find more or as much of it as we can. Once we get some sturdy stakes we can secure these into the ground at the entrance to the doorway. At least then we've got some sort of safety net as everyone can wrap a vine around their waist, attach it to the stake and this will give some level of security and peace of mind to those who feel uneasy. It also gives them a route back.'

James lifts his shoulders: 'Fine by me. Let's get back to the others and tell them our plans.'

As you get back to Mick, Bob, Tracy and Hayley you can see the giant mushrooms tipped upside down leaning against the shortest doorway post. Hayley asks, 'Is everything all right?'

James looks at her and replies: 'Look, we all know this has been stressful, but let's do what we can to help ourselves as well as each other. I think you can tell I'm getting fed up with taking the lead on things, so let's try and share out the responsibility a bit.'

Bob looks across at Mick and mimes to him: 'Is he taking the piss?'

You realise Bob thinks James is feeling a bit too sorry for himself, but you do not want to embroil yourself in an argument so ignore Bob's underhand, silent remark.

The group are looking at the liana which you and James have dragged back. Mick is inquisitive: 'What is that?'

As he points at the long lengths of liana you have tailing behind you both. You respond with confidence: 'This, my friend, is our safety rope. We thought that if we go into this black abyss we can tie some of this liana around our waist, attach it to a stake at the doorway and then at least if we get lost or we are struggling then at least we can make it back.'

Tracy looks up. 'Great idea. I was getting a bit concerned as those gooey mushrooms don't exactly inspire me. Who knows how long they'll hold light for before the stalks snap? And I am not even sure if they will be bright enough down there. Are we definitely doing it then? Are we going in?'

James looks across at you with a telling stare. You know you must tell the group, you must be open and honest with them:

'Look, when I went to get James earlier, we came across a huge waterfall tumbling from a giant expanse of land about half a mile from here. The problem is we are on top of a huge cliff and the only way down to get to the water of the waterfall would either be to abseil using these natural vines or risk going through this doorway in the hope it leads us down.'

Hayley looks at you and James, 'WHAT! Are you joking? There must be another way. We came all the way along here through the forest and that was fine, so there must be a way down without abseiling or going into the unknown?'

You are quick to answer back, 'Well it wasn't exactly fine, was it? I almost lost my life, if you don't remember! I realise you weren't there, but I can tell you it was a scary experience and Bob and me could have easily died yesterday.'

Hayley softens her tone, 'OK, OK, but still, surely there is another option. The idea of tying some long branch type stem around my waist to act as my saviour does not exactly fill me with joy.'

You look around at the group and think the only way to make a fair decision is to give everyone a vote. 'Right let's be democratic about this. Hands up for abseiling down a three hundred feet cliff edge?' You realise you are putting a slightly biased slant on your question, but at least everyone still has an opportunity to show their

preference. No-one raises their hand. So, you continue: 'And who fancies trekking through the forest to see if we can find our way down to the bottom of the waterfall.'

Bob and Mick look at one another: you have gambled that their experiences yesterday would have put them off. Neither put up their hand. Hayley is looking towards Bob, Mick and

James and appears to be put off by their lack of willingness. Tracy is just staring at James intently who stands there motionless.

You quip: 'Well, that's no votes too.' You did not want to appear presumptuous and say that it only leaves the option of going through the doorway. Fortunately, you are saved by Mick and Tracy. Mick initially speaks: 'At the end of the day we went back last night to get the goo and get these mushrooms. It would have been pointless to do this if we were not going to follow through with our initial plan.'

Tracy appears to agree: 'Yeah, to be fair, yesterday we were all up for it. So, let's do it.'

With that Hayley appears resigned to it and stands up from the floor. 'Best go hunting for some of this vine stuff then, shall we?'

You smile at her to show some appreciation towards her willingness to get on with things. You go into the forest as a group and find as much liana as possible before returning to the doorway at around midday.

The sun is scorching hot and the ground is hard, but you start to fashion some pointed stakes with the help of Mick. Everyone is sweating and the lack of water is energy sapping. As you and Mick try to sharpen the points on some chunks of timber, the other four do their best to dig out holes in the hardened mud surrounding the doorway entrance. Working together you secure the posts by late afternoon.

The wooden stakes are in, the liana vines are collected and now you encourage the group to work together in securing it around their waists and around the stakes. James tugs and pulls on his own to check it is secure and both Tracy and

Hayley follow his lead. Mick and Bob check on one another and you ask James to check on yours. The group is ready.

'Ok. Are we ready?' It is a rhetorical question, so you quickly follow up with asking Mick and Bob to carry the goo laden mushrooms through the doorway into the darkness. As the six of you enter through the crooked doorway a hush descends across the group. No-one speaks, there is no wind, no rustling of trees, or plants and even the surface under your feet feels different.

The hard mud you were on outside has gone, it feels as though you are on sand. But you can not see clearly as the glow from the mushrooms is dim. Hayley is right. You turn to the group: 'What do you think we are walking on? It feels like sand. I think I'm paranoid after the other night?'

Mick agrees: 'Yes, definitely sand. The doorway is only 10 metres behind us. I'm going to quickly grab a handful and go back into the sunlight to check.' As Mick turns around there is an almighty bang and a sudden gush of air. The two ladies scream, which in turn makes Bob scream too. 'Aaahhhhhhhhhhhhhhhhh. What's happening?'

It soon becomes apparent that the doorway you have walked through has shut. Mick confirms this as after the initial bang he continues forward and there is no way back out. He shouts from 10 metres away, standing next to what was the open doorway. 'It's solid. It feels like concrete. Surely, it can't be concrete?'

You come back to check what Mick is saying and it is a weird sensation to place your hand against something that feels like polished concrete from a posh office floor or wall. Where had this door come from? You try to place your glowing mushroom around the door and then you realise something. 'Err, folks?'

Bob doesn't need you to carry on, 'I know what you're going to say. Your little idea of us all having these stupid safety cords has been ruined hasn't it.'

Bob tears off the liana vine from around his waist. They had all been severed when the concrete door had shut and threw it onto the floor. 'I knew it. We're doomed!'

Tracy and Hayley look at one another a little confused and then look to James. He says calmly: 'The door, ladies. It has cut all of our safety vines. We've got no way back now.' The ladies start to cry and are hugging one another as James walks over to them. He spreads his long arm around them to comfort them. 'It's OK. We're all still here, we'll be fine.'

James' reassuring words also help you with the situation as you feel a little put out after all the hard work of collecting the vine, making the stakes and convincing the group. You are now feeling out of your depth. You speak to yourself: 'Get a grip.' You need to make this work for the good of everyone. As you meander back to the group with Mick you say: 'We move forward together. Stay close to one another and hold hands if necessary. We're all thirsty and we need to keep our heads.'

You notice, under the dim glow of the translucent mushrooms, that the sand under your feet is dark, grey and ashen. It reminds you of somewhere, but you can't place it in your mind. As you walk forward another 10 metres or so you can feel you are on a slope and decide to share the news. 'We're going downhill, can you feel it? We are on a slope?'

Tracey responds. 'So?'

You add to your initial comment. 'Well, that's what we want. We need to be going down, deeper and deeper to get to the base of the waterfall where we can drink.'

She replies knowingly and slightly embarrassed, 'Yes, of course. Well, that's good, isn't it.'

You all begin walking tentatively forward in the low lighting of the glowing mushrooms. The passage is eerily silent and you want people to talk, but everyone seems too frightened to open their mouths. You are definitely on a slant and the descent feels as though it is getting steeper and steeper. Tracey unexpectedly falls and starts to scream as she whizzes off on her back down the steep incline. You drop your mushroom and just run, following her screams. 'Tracy, Tracy, where are you?'

As you hurtle down the slope her wailing starts to disappear ahead of you. Now you are in a dilemma. Do you carry on running forward or turn around to the safety of the group? You peer back but can only make out slight dots of light. You have made your decision and you start to jog forward, only hearing the sound of your breath.

The temperature has dropped, and you can feel a moisture in the air. Running blind is disconcerting. You felt uncoordinated, frightened and unsure where you are going. There is no noise now in front of you so you keep shouting for Tracy. Then, from nowhere, there is a mighty smack across the side of your face. You fall to the floor and grab your head as you feel a surge of pain running down one side of your face.

You feel huge bristling tentacle type legs and a bulbous squidgy blob. Immediately in your head you think of a squid or an octopus, but you are not in water, so what was it? This creature starts to move across your face and is sucking so hard on your skin that even using all your strength to pull it off is in vain. As you grapple and tug and hit at this thing you realise that between its bristling legs is webbing. The webbing has miniature claws that feel like thorn roses continually pricking into your face. As these mini claws grip your skin the webbing of this creature pulls tight onto your face. The sucking action of the webbing with the pricking action of the tentacles is excruciating beyond belief.

You scream and holler for help, but no-one comes. In your desperation you roll over onto your chest and start to headbutt the floor hoping this will detach the thing smothering your face and head. You feel a slight loosening of the miniature hooks in your cheeks and scalps and quickly grab it with your hands and yank it off. As you throw it into the air the creature hisses and whimpers in an ear-piercing screech.

You cover your ears and in doing so can feel blood dripping from your scalp. You think it is blood, but it is shining; the liquid is bright, luminescent and as you place both your palms on your scalp and remove them your hands glow like beacons of light. The thick gelatinous goo is like slime, like gunk; it is a thick, viscous fluid. And then it dawns on you. This is the same stuff that had been on the leaves. Whatever hideous creature has just attached itself to your head obviously secreted this stuff. Right now, you don't care your hands glow and you can see around five metres ahead of where you point your hands. You keep them straight out left and right like Christ the redeemer on the cross. Your faith is being tested, but now is no time for religion. You just want to survive.

Now you have better peripheral vision and you are able to notice your cavernous surroundings are dingy, dark and dreary. There is little life, but every now and again something scuttles across the dim light you are emitting and this sends a shiver down your spine. You cry out for Tracy: 'Tracy, Tracy can you hear me? If you can, shout.'

The floor has levelled out and so you look around in hope that Tracy must be nearby as she must have come to a halt now that you are no longer on a slope. As you are searching left and right in the cave you hear a distinct, faint murmur which sound like a voice.

You pick up the pace and spring into a jog and begin to stride out and open up the length of your legs into a fast run. You begin to notice markings in the ashen sand beneath your feet. It looks like tire track marks of a car wheel spinning as you notice two distinct black lines, but then you slow and look at the floor beneath you; in between the black lines is a splodge, a thick wider marking in the floor. You stop. It looks like a body has been dragged along the floor.

You look all around and point your glowing hands towards the sky. On the roof of the cave are hundreds of stalactites. Some drip, others glisten, and some remain grey and lifeless. Nothing appears to change as you look up at the dripping stalactites playing a rhythmic drip, tip, tap, tip, tap, tip, tap. The glistening ones shine bright, then dim, shine bright, then dim, whilst the grey and lifeless formations seem to stare and stare and look and stare.

You become entranced with the ceiling of the cave and as

you stare a whistling sound shoots through the air. Before you can move your head to look where the sound has come from you are being dragged along the floor. Your skull hits the ground hard, bang, as your feet are whipped from underneath you. Immediately you grab your head in pain, but you are so badly winded from landing on your back that you gasp for air. The whiplash force at which you have struck the ground has shaken you and you feel disorientated.

As you struggle for breath at the shock you soon realise you are being dragged along the same path you had been looking at only minutes before. You want to scream but your voice doesn't sound as you can hardly catch your breath. All you can feel are two very tightly wound cords around your ankles. You try to reach down, but you are moving so fast your arms are thrown back behind your head.

It is black again. The light from your hands has vanished as the viscous fluid that once stuck to you and glowed has been sheared off as you tried to grab the floor, but to no avail. After what felt like minutes of being dragged forward you feel a sharp movement left which makes your body roll, and as you roll the cords release from your ankles and your back smacks into a wall.

You writhe around in pain as your back feels battered and bruised. The skin on your knuckles, your back, bum and calves feels torn, ripped and as though some-one has sandpapered off the outer layer of your body. You are in so much pain you become delirious and want to vomit, not knowing how to appease the agony.

Then…… splash! Some-one or something threw a bucket of what you assume is ice cold water over you. You shout:

'Ahhh! What's that?'

A voice from the dark replies, 'George, calm down. It's me, Tracy.'

Just hearing her voice is enough. You are pleased she is alive and relieved to have found her, but confused. 'Tracy, where are you?'

She replies quietly, 'I'm over here against the wall, they've shackled me on long chains and I've got two buckets here. One which had water in to drink and to clean, and one for me to go toilet in?'

You immediately try walking in her direction, but as you do an infra-red netting shot up in front on you and gave you a momentary glimpse of Tracy tied to a cave wall in what appear to be medieval type shackles. You try to touch the infra-red netting but it scolds you like boiling water.

Tracy hears you wince: 'Don't bother, they're evil and you need to be careful. You don't know it but I bet you're in one too now.'

You don't understand. 'In what?'

Tracy replies, 'You've been thrown in a cell, but the four walls are invisible. You think I haven't tried to run, tried to escape, scream for help? They got so fed up with me trying they've put these chains on me.'

You need more information: 'Tracy, who are they? Have you seen anyone, heard anything? Where are we?'

She whispers: 'They're not like us, that's all I know. They must have been tracking us though after we walked through that doorway. Maybe it was a trap. I didn't fall on that slope, George. I was taken. I haven't heard them speak, just hissing noises and scratching. When I tried to escape it felt like a million coils were wrapped around me in a split second. I couldn't move. They got tighter as I wriggled so I stopped. As the coils slowly lifted from my arms I just felt the two heavy bracelets slam down on my wrists and the same on my ankles. As the rest of the coils left my body I felt around me to see what I was attached to and felt the chains attached to some sort of cave wall. As I touched around the floor I could feel the two buckets in front of me. One was filled with water and one empty. I've been here for hours George. I'm scared.'

You know it has not been hours, but realise she is in fear of her life. One or two hours at most, but obviously the trauma and horror Tracy has encountered is playing with her mind. You run forward and sure enough, just as Tracy had said, infra-red netting shot down and shot up. As you hit it, it burns your skin.

The soldering smell of sweet pork fills your nostrils: you have burnt the palms of your hands. You turn back in Tracy's direction as you shake your hands vigorously to try and ease the excruciating pain: 'Hey, Trace, you got any of that water left, my hands are sizzling.'

She ushers you back: 'Quick, come here. Follow my voice, but be careful.'

You walk back towards her voice, but you are frightened to get too close as you do not want to fry yourself again. As you get back to where you think you have been before you ask Tracy to shake her chains. 'Hey, Tracy, I don't want to be cooked again. Are you near?'

She replies with haste and you can hear her chain rattle. 'George, just stay where you are and I'll slowly push the bucket towards you.'

You immediately say, 'No, Tracy, the water will come out.'

She replies with disappointment: 'You forget, George, I've already thrown it on you. You will just have to cool your hands on the dampness of the wood. At least it should soothe your skin.'

You feel empty, devoid of optimism. Your back hurts, your face is scarred, your head throbs and now your hands feel on fire. Your desire to help the people you were with has been broken. You fall to the floor in a pile of pain. As you lay in a foetal position you try to think about what you are doing. Why are you here? What has happened to bring you here? Surely the others would come soon enough? You could wait, they would surely find you? What had attacked you and Tracy? Were they going to kill you?

In this last thought it dawns on you that waiting is not an option. You must act now or potentially you could both be dead soon. You drag yourself from the floor and whisper to Tracy: 'I've got an idea, Trace. You said those buckets were wooden. Well...'

You pause, hoping Tracy will understand what you are implying. She replies: 'What?'

You chastise her: 'Come on, Tracy, think!'

Again, she replies: 'What are you on about?'

Frustrated, you explain your idea: 'If they are wooden, they will burn or at least smoulder when they come into contact with the infra-red netting. If they smoulder, the smoke should hopefully show us the infra-red netting and we can try to find its source or any gaps. If they burn then that may attract whatever brought us down here.' Tracy is unimpressed: 'And you think that is a good idea?'

You are not won over by her negativity: 'Have you got any better ones?'

There is a pause and then she replies: 'What are you going to do if you attract whatever dragged us down here? I've already told you about the coils. They have some sort of numinous power. I could feel their presence, but could not see them. The coils. They just wrapped around every part of my body in milliseconds. I was mummified. I mean, what are you going to do, George?'

You sense her anxiousness, but you also think you are in danger. 'You'll have to trust me Tracy. I'm the one who convinced us all to come down here. So I'm the one who is going to get us out. Now, pass me that empty bucket.'

There was no reply. So you repeat her name: 'Tracy.'

Then timidly she says: 'Well, err, yes, ermm.'

You sense all is not right: 'Have you pooed in the empty one?'

She quickly responds: 'No, no, no, but I may have had a little tinkle.'

You laugh and she speaks again: 'Stop it, George. I was scared.'

You sympathise, 'OK, OK, I understand. It's all right. Both the buckets are damp which means they should both smoke or at least steam. Just roll one at a time AND MAKE SURE THEY'RE EMPTY!'

You hear the gentle movement of the ashen sand that lies beneath you, as Tracy walks forward slowly with the wooden buckets in her hand. You can sense her nervousness and want to reassure her. 'Now, be careful. Remember as soon as you see the infra-red appear, move back.' You fall silent and all you can hear is Tracy's nervous breathing and then the buckets dropping as they thud onto the floor. You ask: 'What is it, Tracy?

She responds in anguish: 'George, I can't go any further, my chains won't let me.'

You think for a split second and then say, 'Lay on the floor and try your best to roll them, one at a time. Reach out with your fingertips and then push them away from you as best as you can.'

You visualise Tracy laying prone on the floor with her arms outstretched. You are willing her on in your mind and hoping with all your might that the bucket won't set off the infra-red netting.

Chapter 9

There is an instantaneous flash. You can see the outline of Tracy's body lying outstretched on the floor. The red light flickers around the bucket as it simmers, hisses and starts to smoke. At first you can make out around 5 metres left, right and above the bucket, but as the smoke begins to fill the cave you notice infra-red netting everywhere. After the initial flash you can not see Tracy so you ask her: 'Can you see?'

She replies, hushed and stunned and with a tone of bewilderment: 'It's everywhere.'

You are looking around frantically trying to store the image of where the netting is around you, but it appears to go on and on and deep into the cave. There appears to be different tunnels and you are trying to situate yourself and where you had come from and then you stop. You gulp. You don't move. You stare.

Something huge looms in the distance. You know it is big as it appears to black out the infra red netting near the top of one of the cave tunnels. You know these tunnels are at least five metres tall. This 'thing' moves slowly up the tunnel, ominously; with intent, it seems to stop every other second and search around.

You remain motionless. Murmuring to Tracy you say: 'Stay down, don't move.'

In your head whatever is moving towards you is at least ten to fifteen metres wide and at least five metres tall. It is huge, but is moving slowly and is quiet. As it gradually gets closer, you have an idea. 'Tracy, quick, get the other bucket.' You hear her scurry off in the sand and on her return, she asks: 'Now what?'

You reply: 'On my command put it in the infra-red. I'm hoping it will cause a flash of light and surprise whatever that thing is coming towards us. I'm warning you though, I may be grabbing both of those buckets soon as I don't want to hang around and find out what this beast is all about. Now, steady yourself and wait for my command.'

As the beast looms ever larger the infra-red netting covering the different areas of the cave is absorbed into its thick black globular mass of a body. You can no longer see the tunnels which the infra-red netting has highlighted as this thing moves ever closer. You start to hear a whipping, swooshing, zipping sound and then – CRACK!!! A rope-like tentacle whizzes past your face and crashes into the wall that Tracy is attached too. You shout: 'Now, Tracy!'

She follows your command and puts the second wooden bucket into the last remaining infra red netting that you can see in the cave. Whooosh – there is a flash of light just like before. The infra netting cackles momentarily and becomes fuzzy. In a moment of madness you jump through it to be with Tracy. Doing so you scald your forearms, shins and part of your chin, but you make it through. You quickly grab Tracy from the floor: 'Quick. Get against the wall.'

As Tracy runs to the wall that she was attached to with chains, another thunderous lashing sound whizzes through the air in close proximity. You shout: 'Get down, Tracy.' She cowers on the floor next to the wall in a ball, clutching her head and pushing her knees to her chest. You hear shards of rock tumble from the wall as this beast launches yet another tentacle.

You have a plan. Grabbing both of the buckets you run back to Tracy and then, in a split second, throw them as high as you can. The infra-red netting is not visible so you just hope the buckets will hit it at the same time and cause a big enough flash to see what is in front of you.

You throw with every ounce of energy you have. The buckets set off the infra-red netting with a giant flash. The creature becomes clear for a fleeting second. It has what appears to be around twenty tentacles, or appendages, or feelers, or antennae; you don't know what they are as they lash around at the front of a huge, globular body, like that of an octopus. They are all different thicknesses; some appear like the cables on common plugs, whilst others are much thicker in diameter. You were imagining rope as thick and round as a jam jar.

All the tentacles, or appendages, or feelers, or antennae or whatever they are come spiralling out, reaching between ten to twenty metres and recoiling back into the beast. The flash of light appears to distract this thing before you and the whipping and slashing become wild. First left, then right, up and down. As soon as you throw the buckets up you run forward towards the beast. You jump across the infra-red webbing, but no pain this time as you are filled with adrenaline and dive to the floor with your arms outstretched. You have managed to wedge yourself under the belly of the beast.

You dare not move and all you can feel is a giant balloon

type cushion pressured above your head and shoulders. This colossal creature cuts an ominous figure, but you are now buried underneath it and safe from its tentacles which you can still hear whirling and whizzing through the underground cave.

Immediately you think of Tracy's safety and turn your prone body around so that your face is now pressed against the underbelly of the beast. You think to pierce its skin to distract it from Tracy's direction but nothing on the sandy floor is sharp. You then think about your own finger nails: they are sharp, uncut and probably ragged enough to inflict some sort of pain. As you dig your fingers into the skin of the beast it feels gelatinous and spongey. You press and press and there is no reaction. Then, in an instant, the beast lifts from your body and you hear a repetitive metal clanging sound. The next thing you hear is Tracy: 'George, get back here. NOOOOOOOOOOOWWWWW!!!' You rush back towards her and notice there is no infra-red netting.

You wonder what is going on, why she is panicking: 'What is it, Trace?'

'It's doing what it did to me....... it's covering itself in coils. I can just tell, it's the same sound and can you smell it?'

As you inhale through your nostrils there is a distinct smell, but you thought metals do not usually smell on their own. Then you realise what the smell is: the buckets have continued to smoulder and burn and perhaps this has caused some sort of reaction to the beasts own breathing mechanism. Perhaps you entering the cave system has increased the levels of carbon dioxide enough to draw its attention. This makes you think, was the beast protecting itself, had it tried to protect Tracy?

The once bulbous, globular, orbicular blob is now a rigid, firm, uniform structure and you envision its transformation from some sort of giant octopus to a huge cross between an armadillo and pangolin.

The beast does not move and so you quickly bash and smash the chains holding Tracy to the cave wall with the still smouldering buckets. One of the attachments to the wall has loosened so you heave and tug with all your power and two long screws come tumbling out of the wall and you begin to cough and choke as the rock dust fills your lungs. With one hand free, Tracy begins to yank at the other chain and after spluttering and wheezing onto the floor you crawl round to her other side to help. You place your legs on the cave wall in a rowing position, with one leg either side of the chain and pulled and pulled with all your might. This time there is nothing. Tracy pleads with you: 'Come on, don't give up, we need to get out of here before that thing wakes up.'

Her timing is perfect as the beast jolts and shudders, and as its coiled body unravels from it foetal position it clanks and reverberates like an old medieval knight of the realm getting ready for a jousting competition.

You immediately stand up and as you face towards the clattering sounds two sharp, ruby-red dots stare back at you. Two red dots appear on your forehead and you only know this because Tracy is hysterical: 'Ahhhhh, we're going to die, George. George, do something, we're going to die! He's going to kill you, George; do something. You've got laser dots on your forehead, George; do something.'

Your initial reaction is to touch your forehead, but then

you duck and momentarily you look behind and see the dots flash onto the wall.

The imminent danger Tracy feels is not the same emotion in you. You are calm and thinking at a thousand miles per hour. Why had the beast not moved towards you, why had it unravelled itself, why had it not attacked Tracy? All these questions make you consider the beast did not want to kill or attack, it wanted to protect and locate you. You move towards it slowly and notice the laser beams are now on your chest. You continue forward and the beams move to your hips and then to your feet. You are being scanned.

You are walking like a zombie, slowly and with your arms in front of you in the pitch-black darkness. The reverberating clanging sounds have stopped, but every now and then you can make out the squeaking and shrill sound of metal rubbing against metal. With your palms open flat, your soft skin touches a cold metallic surface. You are touching the beast.

You think about what you are touching and start to pat gently around to decipher the shape of the beast. You begin to think that a beast is descriptive of a scary, aggressive and potentially dangerous animal. Is this a beast? An almighty hissing sound makes you cover your ears as two streams of hot gas shot out from what you were touching onto the ashen sand floor. You then hear Tracy shout from behind you, 'George, are you all right? What's happening?'

She is wailing in despair and so you want to calm her angst: 'It's OK, Trace, I don't think it's going to hurt us.'

Tracy is blubbering and clearly in distress: 'But, George, it tied me to a cave wall for goodness sake, it's not friendly!'

You know in Tracy's mind that what you are doing is madness. But you have an inkling, an intuitive sense, this thing, this giant creature, is was no beast, this is an underground being scared and trying to protect itself and now you think it is trying to protect you too.

You take a step towards the streams of gas that had ejected so rapidly and stroke what you assume is a nose. In doing so a nozzle of over one hundred rings rattle through your hands at electric speed. The first few rings feel no bigger than a wedding ring, but they increase with size and stop coming out from the creature when they have reached the spherical diameter of a drinking glass.

'George, George.' Tracy is shouting for your attention. 'George, the shackles on my wrists and ankles, George, they're loosening.'

You smile. Now it is time to find the others.

Chapter 10

'Tracy, come here and check this out.'

You are feeling around the body of the metallic creature and can feel levers and buttons.

'I don't know, George. We don't want to upset it.'

You think about Tracy's comment: 'If it wanted to kill us, we'd be dead already.'

With that you pull down on a lever and hear something pop loudly. Tracy yells: 'What was that?'

You both start to feel around this huge being, trying to deduce what is happening. 'Up here, Tracy.'

You have managed to climb up the nozzle from the front onto what must have been its head.

As you get to the top of the creature you bang your head on the cave roof and yelp in pain. This scares Tracy: 'You OK, George, what's happening?'

You need to keep communicating with her as you sense her helplessness: 'I'm fine Tracy, I think I'm on top of the creature and I just banged my head on the roof of the cave.'

You diligently feel around and come across a flat, erect piece of metal, one side of an incomplete box as you reach around and feel two more identical sides. It feels as though there are three sides of an old computer monitor, or really old large TV. The back and two sides, but no front.

'Tracy.' You spoke quite loudly. 'Tracy, I've found something.'

She replies, scared: 'George, please come down, I'm frightened.'

You are caught in two minds, as you want to see what is inside the three small walls of metal. As you reach around them to the front there is nothing but then your hand slips forward. A hole. 'Tracy, I'm going in.'

It is a difficult decision as you recognise Tracy is scared, frightened and feeling vulnerable, but you need to see. She cries out to you: 'Where are you going, George?'

You need to reassure her: 'I'll be quick, Tracy. I think I can go into this creature, I'll be out really soon.'

The hole is tight, the width only just enough to fit your hips through. As you dangle your feet over the lip of the hole you feel a gooey substance not much thicker than water. You wriggle and jiggle and jostle and squirm until you are fully immersed with only your head appearing out of what feels like a square drain hole.

The liquid you are in was warm. It feels soothing and your muscles are being squeezed and relaxed like a deep tissue massage. You have to make a decision whether or not to submerge your head.

You go for it. At first, after dunking your head, you close your eyes, but as you open them the surroundings are familiar. Wispy clouds, streaks of dusty light, specks of gold flash and then, as you swivel your body, you begin to dive towards two flashing lights. You think they may be the ruby-red lasers that had scanned you previously.

As you got near towards the strawberry red lights they begin to flutter and turn lighter to a bubblegum pink which sparkles and glistens and shines. You are drawn closer in amazement and two fairies flutter in front of you.

'Do you know who we are, George?'

You vaguely recognise them. One has flowers behind her ear, the other flowers woven around her feet and ankles in a delicate daisy chain. You can not think straight and then the angels speak in unison: 'Who are you?'

The angels again speak in an unnerving unison, 'We are Rose and Dandelion. You came to us in a time of need in a previous incarnation of your life. You think you have forgotten, but you are still you, George. You even named yourself George because this is who you are. There have been many transformations in your life, many you cannot remember, you do not wish to remember. You have suppressed so much, George – rightly so. We helped you before and we will help you again. George, believe.'

You try desperately to place the angels in your mind. As you float there, deep in thought, they flutter away through two small holes which you fathom are the holes that the lasers had come from. You know you have seen them, but just can't recall them from your past. The angels left a trail of sparkling dust which drew your gaze. You follow the specks, fall deeper and deeper and as you follow you notice below you a bright, twinkling, gleaming light amongst the hazy, ghostly, purple mist around you.

You go towards it and there is a golden bee vibrating fiercely on a golden glistening leaf. The bee does not move, it just vibrates and you feel a surprising urge to grasp it. As you grab at the bee you feel it writhe and twist and buzz in your hand, but it does not sting. The golden leaf which has been floating on its own, suspended in the haze, rapidly breaks up like a withering, bristling, ancient autumn leaf. Its remnant parts drift away in the mist that surrounds you and appears to evaporate into the haze. Where were you?

The lack of skeleton or organs inside the beast soon dawn on you. No spine, no ribs, no heart, no lungs, no liver, no kidney and most important…….. no brain! How had this thing moved, how had it tied up Tracy, what were the infra-red webs?

You suddenly remember Tracy is outside quivering in fear and you quickly swim back up to the square you had entered. Hauling yourself out you make sure the dazzling bee remains tight in your clasp. You shout: 'Tracy, are you still down there?'

She shouts up: 'Yeah, hurry up though, I'm getting cold and want to get out of here.'

You lower yourself down and start to explain how the insides of the creature are missing, but you don't tell Tracy about the fairies inside.

As your hand vibrates you open your grip ever so slightly and a ray of light shoots out into the darkness. Tracy looks immediately at your right hand and clenched fist: 'What's in there?'

You don't know what to say, so blurt out: 'Oh, urm, I found this light thingy-majiggy inside the creature and err…'

Tracy is too disorientated to care for your response and is already walking towards the light. She looks back at you: 'Let's walk back up to find the others.'

Almost as soon as she finishes talking a glow appears on top of the brow of the slope which led to you. Tracy looks at you with excitement in her eyes: 'It must be them.'

You start shouting: 'Down here, come down here, but watch your footing, that slope is slippery.'

You put your arm round Tracy and she puts both of hers around your waist as gradually the group start to walk down the slope towards you. There is a palpable sense of relief as the group rejoined and Hayley is quick to mention the outline of the giant creature behind you.

'What the hell is that?'

Tracy responds, 'Don't ask, let's just get out of here!'

With that you start to walk around the left side of the now stationary creature. James, Mick and Bob bombard you with questions, most of which you parry back and give little detail as you are still figuring things out in your own mind.

The fairies, the hazy mist, the golden flecks, the bee in your hand and the grey, dark ashen sand you walked upon. All were familiar, but you couldn't place them. As you walk, Tracy, who had been chatting to Hayley and James, called across: 'Hey, George, what was that light in your hand?'

Damn it, you think. She hasn't forgotten and now you have to make up a story to the others or you could tell the truth? Why aren't you telling the truth? What is your fear. Then you remember Bob's wariness towards you when you first joined the group and you question your own friendship with James. Would he be annoyed if you hid things from him? As these thoughts cross your mind, you look at Tracy and see the innocence in her eyes. She wants the truth and deserves the truth, but it sounds so farfetched. You decide to wait till later.

James luckily spoke soon after Tracy and he veers the conversation to something more important: getting out and getting water. 'Have you noticed how much colder it's getting and can you smell the air. It's musty. I think we're deep and I reckon it won't be too much further till we're at the bottom. We must have been trekking downwards now for at least two or even three hours.'

You respect James' judgement; he speaks with authority, distinction, and clarity. James is articulate, and the group would go quiet when he speaks in his deep dulcet tones. The old crooner Barry White could easily have been his brother, but James was far leaner and lankier than the famous singer. James is still just as silky smooth with his velvety tones. And as he speaks the ladies ogle at him and hang on his every word.

Mick, Bob and I listen intently as we know whatever comes out of his mouth always has purpose. James knows all of this and strides around with confidence. His long, languorous stride often means others have to walk fast to keep up. He knows this and he asserts his physical presence as well as his clear-thinking mind.

There is an attractiveness to James' confidence, and you feel slightly jealous in the way the women swoon after him. You have respect though and he has confided in you, so when he speaks you listen along with the group. James gives his thoughts: 'I think it would be best if we veered right, with all these tunnels it is difficult to choose, but from where we entered I believe we have come relatively straight and thinking about where George and I spotted the water earlier it would make sense to start heading right.'

You think about what James had just said and in your mind agree with his suggestion. As a group you set off right, down another dark tunnel, but you have an instinctive fear that something is following you so you keep on looking behind. The others notice your constant head turning and Bob angrily asks: 'What is it with you, George. Every two seconds you're looking behind as though something is coming. You're making us feel nervous.'

You give an honest reply: 'Look, we've come down the tunnel on the right which I agree would make sense. However, when Tracy and I were together that giant creature up there came out of one of the tunnels on the left. I'm just worried we could be set upon at any moment.'

Hayley, who is holding the hand of Tracy, does not appreciate your comment: 'Shut up George, I'm frightened enough and just want to get out of here. Keep your stupid thoughts to yourself.'

James tries to stop the bickering: 'Ssshh, everybody, I can hear water.'

You all fall silent and can hear a swishing sound, you recognised the sound and try to place it in your mind. You had heard it before when you had been in the tunnel with the maid, but that memory was not with you now. There is only the faint recollection of a similar experience.

Mick shudders you from your daze: 'Look, some sort of port hole. Bob, hold the lamp.' With his bulging biceps and brute strength Mick starts to pull with all his power onto a lever attached to the spherical metal drain lid.

You looked around and shout: 'Stop, stop! Bob, what happens if water comes rushing in here? This cave tunnel could fill up real quick and we'd have nowhere to turn.'

As though watching a tennis match, the group's eyes shoot from right to left. Mick, on the right, is pulling on the lever, you on the left of the group are shouting at him to stop. The group then quickly avert their gaze back to the right to ensure Mick has stopped yanking at the lever. Not a word is said as everyone turns left back to you. In response, you quickly press your index finger against your pursed lips to indicate silence. The group then look right again, but this time it is not at Mick but over his broad hanger-like shoulders.

The spherical metal lid is creaking, moaning, popping, squealing. You shout, 'Move, move, move. It's going to blow!' You start to run back up the tunnel and the others chase you, dropping the mushroom lanterns behind them. There is an almighty BANG! The metal lid has exploded off the wall from the immense pressure it was under from holding back the water. Mick has loosened it enough that it can no longer take the enormous volume of water pressing on it.

As it bursts through there is a voluminous vortex of vivacious water which bubbles, swirls and gushes at cheetah speed up the tunnel. You are sprinting like a gazelle, but the cheetah is fast approaching. Pumping your arms and driving your knees you are shouting crazed encouragement at the others: 'Quickly, quickly, hurry up.'

The sound of the water crashing, smashing and vaulting off the walls is getting louder and louder. You imagine a hungry coalition of cheetahs chasing down a herd of gazelles. As the water springs from the sides of the tunnel and pounds along the floor, your legs become heavier as your lungs start to rupture with exhaustion.

As you look behind Bob is not with the group. You scream to the others: 'Stop stop! Where's Bob?'

There is an eruption of noise and you are lifted off your feet in a dark liquid mass. You hold onto your head and tuck your knees to your chest as you are buffeted and pummelled between the walls, ceiling and floor of the tunnel. You know that you have been walking on a slight slope downwards so hang on to the hope that the water will eventually stop flowing up.

As you bounce, flounder, flail and flap you can feel the others as soft squidgy forms in the water, which you softly bump against before drifting off in different directions. You try to remain calm as you know you are at the behest of the raging torrents which threw you back up into the cave system. You can do nothing and calmly accept your fate that you will soon die through drowning.

This thought abruptly halts your tranquillity. You panic. You don't want to drown, to perish in pain as your lungs fill with water rather than air. You swim hard, you swim with the current and you swim for your life.

Again, the feintest of memories flashes through your mind, but you have no time to recall previous encounters of almost drowning through exhaustion. You decide to swim as high as you can, but clatter your head on a stalactite. Although you can not see, you know you are bleeding as your immediate reaction is to grasp your head in pain and you can feel your torn scalp with fluid oozing from the flappy skin.

You re-focus and dive down a little to avoid getting struck again. When you peer back up from beneath the water you realise the cavities between the stalactites could provide pockets of air. Quickly, you go a little higher but flow with the current whilst raising both hands in the air. You look like a horizontal Frankenstein drifting in water, blood flowing from your head. The back of your hands brusquely clatters a dripping rock and so you quickly turn to face the current and thrash around vainly trying to find what you had hit. You strike it again. Excitedly, you hang on to stalactite praying it will not snap from the roof of the cave tunnel.

You heave yourself up with the last remnants of energy in your body. The stalactite is getting wider and you wish upon hope that you are nearing the roof. Then, in a blissful realisation, you can feel a minute gap, a crevice, and quickly thrust your nose and lips into the tiny opening.

Panting for air your thoughts turn to the others. Had they thought of the same idea? Surely James, but what about the others? You are caught in a quandary whether to go back under and flow with the current or just stay floating with this pocket of air keeping you alive. As you pontificate on your predicament you try to turn your head so that your ear protrudes from the water in place of your mouth and nose. At least this way you may be able to make out any cries or shouts from the others.

Unfortunately, this wishful thinking as you knock your head again and wince with pain, but even though you are able to ascend sideways to lift your ear, all you can hear on the surface of the water is the rapturous torrent of cascading up into the cave. The continuous dripping from the cave roof fills your ear, whenever you try to escape the water to listen for the others. As you alternate between breathing and trying to listen you notice the water levels are subsiding. The flow of water is weakening and perhaps the diminishing flow means that the levels of water are dropping in the tunnel. As your brain rushes through a thousand decisions, an alarm goes off in your frontal lobe.

You feel an immense guilt when realising the bee you had retrieved from the murky depths of the creature in the tunnel is still in your tightly bound fist. Had it drowned? Surely you had killed it? You feel horrible, but have no way of knowing if the bee is still alive as you dare not open your hand and expose the bee to the rushing water.

Then you have an idea: the bee shone light like a lighthouse beam emanating from the murky depths inside the giant creature of the tunnel. Surely, if the bee is still alive you could release it and hope that the golden beam it emitted may guide the others to dry land. It is a whimsical idea, but in your panic-stricken state you just think the bee would want to stay dry and would find its own way. Your tenuous thought process is that the others will see this glow and follow the light in the darkness that surrounds them.

You submerge yourself into the water and whilst holding onto the stalactite with one hand you reach up and release the bee into the pocket of air you had been breathing from. You close your eyes and pray.

You feel the bee leave your hand and flutter furiously away. As you plunge back into the water you try to grip the stalactite so that you can heave yourself to the surface again for air.

This time, as you haul yourself upwards, the stalactite snaps, and the shock causes you to inhale sharply and you began to choke on water. You kick frantically to try and keep your position in the fast-flowing waters, but you are pulled hurriedly along by the current. Your face is pummelled with gritty pieces of rock and stone floating around the water after pieces of the cave wall and ceiling had become loose. This is it. Your time is up. You let the water roll over you and close your eyes.

Chapter 11

Are you dead? You look around and it's dark, but you can sense light in the distance. Are you in heaven?

You hear water crashing nearby and then voices. 'George, George. Guys, he's moving.' Hayley is hysterical, but all you can see through your blurry vision is the outline of five bodies looming over you. They are all fuzzy and you are still coming in and out of consciousness. You can feel somebody kneel close to your face. A deep voice whispers, 'Come on now, George, we've come this far, you can't give up on us now.'

You recognise the velvety, soft tones of James' voice and it makes you believe you are alive. It comforts you as your head is spinning and your body feels numb with pain.

You move your head to the side without knowing your nose is pressed against James' nose. You murmur: 'I'm trying.' This is all you can muster as you fall back into a black chasm of unconsciousness. All of those who had ventured into the cave with you had survived the rush of water. Mick, Bob, James, Hayley and Tracy were all blown back into the cave and have all managed to swim to safety onto a plateau of grey ashen sand. They have waited for you anxiously, believing you were dead as you hung to the stalactite not knowing that the rest of the group were safe.

Tracy had told the others to shush when you were calling as she thought she could hear your voice amongst the crescendo of the water thrashing around the cave. She was right, but it did not matter as you did not hear anything back. Now they wait and pray for you to come around again.

James and Hayley stay close by to ensure you are breathing as the others talk about the light. Not the light from the cave wall, but a flashing light they had all witnessed, a golden light which left a blur like a sparkler at Halloween, a tail of light which flashed and bounced across the cave walls before exiting through the hole Mick had accidently created. As they talk you realise you are listening to their conversation. You are intrigued as the bee in your hand has survived; it has escaped the water and flown to the bottom of the waterfall.

You sit up quickly. Your eyes bulging. 'We must follow the bee.'

Hayley strokes your head: 'George, honey, you're delirious, there's no bees in here.' You are annoyed at her dismissive response. 'You don't understand that light they are talking about. That light is our saviour. That light is what we must follow. I am that light, I was holding it and it was keeping me alive in those waters; as soon as I let go I came to you guys, alive. I believe in the light and the light is a bee.

Bob looks at you: 'A bee? How does a bee save you, swim in water and become a light? An all hailing saviour of a light at that! I think you banged your head harder than you think!'

You reply sharply, 'Bob, you're going to have to trust me. You were right in the past and your intuition has been spot on. At the fire when we first met, then when we returned to the forest and now, you were right again...... it was dangerous to come down here. On all accounts your gut feeling was right.

'However, I'm telling you now to trust me and I'm telling the truth because I know the truth. I was holding a golden bee, a special bee which I've held before. They are the true light and gold as you think you know it comes from the death of these bees over millions of years. That precious shiny shimmering glorious gold that ruled our world is born from the amalgamation of billions of these bees crushed together in the earth over thousands of years. It sounds ridiculous, but these bees have power.'

Bob rolls his eyes in disbelief and walks away from where the group is gathered. Mick looks over at you lying on the floor: 'Hey George, I like you man, you're a good guy. But bees? Come on, dude, you've got to give us more than that.'

Your mind is clear, it is as if the unconsciousness has stirred the neurological networks in your brain and your memories are flooding back, but you are cute enough to choose what you say to the group. Telling them you have witnessed the bees cut beneath the earth's crust to help you turn the land masses of the world is perhaps not the best thing to say at this juncture.

You look Mick square in the eyes, noticing for the first time his giant, angular head and thick foreboding neck. 'Mick, I love you, man, you've trusted me from day one and never questioned my ideas.' You pause and make inferences towards Bob with your eyebrows, highlighting his lack of faith in you along this journey. You say to Mick: 'And now, more than ever, I really need you brother. Stay with me, trust in me and we will be OK. I beg you.'

Mick's giant head is looking at the floor, but your impassioned speech seems to raise his eyes from his furrowed brow. 'OK, man, what's your next suggestion to get us out of this mess?'

You turn to everybody and ask: 'You were talking about the

bee or, OK, you were talking about this flashing whirring light. Where did you say it went again?'

Hayley replies in a shot, 'Straight out of the cave wall.'

She pauses and then jokingly says, 'You know, through the giant hole Mick created!'

James and Tracy laugh and Mick smiles, but Bob is still stood away from everyone and remains silent. You stand up and in a firm voice proclaim: 'Right then, let's follow that light out of here. Anyone want to come?

And with that you run towards the shadowy waters, dive in and swim towards the direction of the hole in the cave wall.

After about ten strokes it dawns on you that not everybody might be able to swim. You stop. Treading water, you are not sure how deep the cave is. You begin to shout back towards the others. 'Hello, Tracy, Hayley, Bob? Can anyone hear me?'

You can make out some splashing noises and some panting so you continue to tread water. The first person to crash into you is Mick.

'Whoa there!' you exclaimed, as if trying to pacify a disobedient horse.

'Sorry, I couldn't see anything.'

Mick apologises in his thick Latvian accent for his awkward arrival in the murky waters. Following him, the two ladies are breast stroking and chatting about how they used to swim at their local pools. You assume they are trying to distract themselves from the lingering fear of being in a dark, damp, cold and eerie cave. James is gasping frantically as he approaches you, spluttering as he speaks: 'I can't stop, I'm freezing and can't swim very well, so just want to get out of here.'

You let him go and encourage the others to swim with him.

You continue to wait for Bob, but hear nothing. You decide to swim back.

As you approach the land from which you have set off from you call out after him: 'Bob, Bob, are you here?'

From the shadows and depths of the cave you hear a distant reply: 'What do you want?'

You can sense he is angry, but you ask him anyhow: 'Are you not coming?'

Bob's voice becomes louder as you make out a sinister, shadowy figure walking towards you: 'Time and time again I've gone along with the crowd. I've followed your instructions. James' instructions. Listened to Mick, agreed with the girls. Well, not this time. This time I've had enough!'

You can sense Bob is angry and annoyed so don't want to incense him anymore. 'OK, Bob, I agree, your voice needs to be heard. What should we do?'

There is a bit of silence. Then Bob says: 'Well, I'd already started walking back when you turned up. I think if we walk back to where we found you and Tracy we should look towards taking another tunnel.'

You take Bob's point on board and pause to show you are thinking about it. You disagree, but tactfully respond:

'How are we going to go up there, Bob? Isn't it pitch black? And remember that beast? Surely you don't want to risk another one of them? I'm with you though. If you want to walk back I'll follow you.

Bob replies, 'Let's go then.'

You were not expecting that response. He has called your bluff and with most of the group now swimming in the opposite direction, towards the hole in the wall, you have to think fast. You ask, 'What way we headed then, Bob?'

The double bluff. There is noticeable silence and hesitancy to his response. It makes you realise that Bob is actually just annoyed and was letting off steam. He didn't have a plan, he was just angry. Bob replies hastily:

'I don't bloody know, do I. You got us into this mess and now I'm stuck here!'

You pick up on Bob's emphasis on the words 'I'm stuck here'. There was no 'we're stuck here' and you gain a feeling that he is scared. It comes to you. Bob couldn't swim. You ask him outright. 'Bob, what's wrong? Can you not swim?'

Clearly angered, Bob replies: 'No, I bloody can't. And you, you ignorant imbecile, you dived straight in without a thought.'

You empathise, but want to explain your presumption:

'But Bob, you've been at sea catching fish, catching whales, I just, you know, I just assumed!'

With a slightly calmed voice, Bob replies: 'Exactly. You just assumed. You assumed I didn't notice you appearing from thin air that night at the fire. You assumed it was a good idea to go back into the forest to collect that goo. What about the assumption that this was the quickest way to get to fresh water! Your assumptions appear to be making an ASS out of U and ME too in this instance!'

You lower your own voice and calmly speak: 'You're right, Bob, and I'm sorry. I promise you I've only ever been trying to help and I'm sorry if I've imposed my will upon the group in a negative way. I really am as desperate as everyone else to find some safety and some water.'

Bob appears to appreciate your contrite response and

follows it by saying, 'OK, lad. Look, we're in a bit of a pickle here. I don't really fancy going back up there.' Bob is pointing towards the darkness of the cave from which you have walked down, but you can not see his hand. 'Nor do I want to be back in those freezing waters. Whenever I went out to see, I tethered any floating debris I could find to me so that if I was to fall in I knew that I would bob up and down. Do you get it, 'bob up and down?'

As Bob laughs at his own rubbish joke you chuckle along with him and the ice is broken. You can feel him talking on a calmer plane and offer him a suggestion. 'Look, I know I've been wrong in the past, but we've worked together and got this far and we're all still alive. I used to be a lifeguard many years ago, I'm a strong swimmer and, if you will let me, I'll drag you out that hole.'

Bob retorts, 'How do you intend on doing that then?'

With his response you know you are pushing at an open door. Bob has shown he is open to your proposal, so you realise you better make it a good one. 'We'll walk in together and once we're in you need to lay facing up so that you can breath and I'll lay underneath you. The buoyancy provided by the water will help me carry you. I'll clasp your chin and you just need to keep your hips high and lift your bum. Kick if you can. I'll drag your head by pulling your chin. Bob, we can do this.'

Bob is apprehensive. You give him a clear authoritative instruction. 'I'm going to clasp your chin. Just wait until we're in there, you'll see.'

So, you walk into the water together and you encourage Bob to lay back. You wrap your left arm under his back and wrap your right arm over his chest and hold onto his chin with your right hand. In unison and with you leading the momentum, you splash back into the water.

'Bob, Bob, just say something, anything.'

Bob's words are to the point; he chokingly splutters, 'Swim you idiot.'

You swim as fast but as fluidly as you can. Pulling Bob by the chin you are breast stroke kicking with your legs and keeping your own head out of the water whilst shouting at him to reassure him. 'Keep kicking, Bob. You're doing well. We're almost there.'

You are excited as the hole in the cave comes closer and closer, but as you approach it the current beneath your body becomes stronger. You respond by kicking with more power. You are exhausted and feel weak with fatigue, but know that for you and Bob to stay alive it requires both of you to kick. You yell at him to kick harder, but you have nothing left and yet you are so close to the exit.

There is a thunderous sound as you emerge ever so slowly from the cave to an almighty waterfall cascading over the rocks high above the ground. The midday sun blinds you momentarily. You quickly glance around look for land as the waters froth and bubble and fizz, absconding your view. Then, through the midst and spray, you can hear the shouts and cries of the others. You head towards their cries and are relieved when Mick and Tracy dive in to help you drag Bob to the rocks at the base of the waterfall.

Chapter 12

T he water is crystal clear and glints in the sunlight. You cup your hands and drink. It is divine. The others are splashing around and enjoying their first taste of fresh water in days. The water is icy cold, but that doesn't seem to stop their frivolity as they played joyously in the midday glare of the sun. You sit on a nearby rock and watch the group laughing and playing together and, for the first time in days, you smile. As you grin, Hayley shouts over to you: 'Come on, George, come join us.'

You don't even think and dive into the fresh stream which runs around two hundred metres down from the waterfall. As you blithely wallow and wade in the stream you lay on your back to soak up the sense of joy and happiness you can hear all around with the others laughing and cavorting with one another. As the afternoon ends, you make camp at the side of the river and a full moon lights the night sky.

In the starry, clear skies above you hear a rustling in the woodland near the back of the camp-fire. You stand up instantly with your index finger pressed against your pursed lips. Ushering everyone else to stay seated and silent you already see James moving stealthily into the darkness. You follow close behind and notice James holding a javelin-like spear above his right shoulder, his biceps poised to unleash the pointed stick in his grasp.

There is a rustle, a snort and then a squeal, which pierces

the silence of the night and makes your heart shudder with anguish. James had unleashed his spike into the spine of an unsuspecting and frightened wild boar. As you rush towards the animal James is knelt across it's back slitting its throat with a sharpened stone. You turn to him: 'Mate, you city bankers sure are ruthless. Where did you learn those Neanderthal skills?'

He stares at you in the grey light of the night. 'George, my friend, I come from the Igbo tribe, a warrior clan, where survival skills are a rite of passage. These scars you see on my cheeks, they show I'm a survivor. We had to spend two weeks in the wilderness as 13-year-old boys and come back to our villages alive.'

You look at the boar and the pool of blood it is now lying in. James starts laughing. 'If you believe that mumbo jumbo, you'll believe anything. George, I'm a practical guy and we need to eat. Are you not starving? I was praying for food this evening as I had tried up stream to catch fish all afternoon, but to no avail. I was desperate and thank God this pig came into our camp.'

The crisp, crackling sound of fat is joined with the succulent aroma of sizzling bacon. What a smell. You can feel your mouth salivating as the searing pork perfume perforates the clear air around you.

Mick is the first to chew on the hardened outer skin of the boar and you watch in slow motion as fat drizzles from his carnivorous jaws and slowly drips from the sides of his mouth. Mick doesn't care, he is ravenous, and it is not long before everyone is joining in.

Ripping and tearing at the meat of the roasting beast which

James had turned diligently for the past hour. There is little to no appreciation as the hunger of everyone takes over and it becomes a voracious feeding ground for all. You grin to yourself as you watch Hayley, 'the pescatarian' who had vehemently espoused the virtues of her non-meat consumption, chomping down the juiciest piece of pork you can imagine. That night everyone slept well.

In the morning, there is a whiff of smoky charcoal mixed with pork, it brings back memories of the heavenly feast from the night before and makes your stomach rumble. As each person groggily arises from their meat-induced coma there is a silent contentment and acknowledgement of happiness between everybody.

Smiles and grins pass around the grey ashes of the previous night's fire. Everyone has been well fed, has enjoyed a calm and tranquil sleep and feels safe. The fear of having no water, no food and no light has evaporated. A new dawn and a new adventure is just around the corner. Your mind is crystal clear, your vision is sharp, you are focussed and ready to go. You summon the group: 'Right, we're going to follow the water, it's our source of survival and it must be the source for others too. If we follow the current we might find other survivors.'

No-one speaks and you take that as a sign of agreement. As you lead the group away from the burnt-out camp fire you feel energised and invigorated. Kapooow, bam, kazaam! you start punching the air and saying silly things to yourself as you exude an inner belief that reverberates around the group. Everyone is walking at a brisk pace, smiling to one another and talking enthusiastically about the real possibility of finding other people. This contagious, positive emotion is enhanced through the bright blue sky. There is not a cloud to be seen and the glowing sun emanates a radiant heat that warms the swirling breeze around the river bank.

Leaves bristle on the trees that surrounded you and then it hits you. Why was there a breeze, but no cloud? This is weird. This doesn't feel right. You don't want to quash the positive vibes of the group, but your joyous morning was beginning to feel jaded already. Something doesn't feel right and it puts you on edge.

'George, George.' Tracy and Hayley are shouting in unison, grabbing at each other's arms. They are staring into the woods. 'George, what's that? Something's looking at us.'

You investigate the dense woodland and can not see anything, so try to ease their fears. 'Are you two hallucinating, or are you still reminiscing, Tracy. Come on, you two, pull yourselves together, there's nothing following us. We're the hunters now!'

You carry on walking but feel the pace of the group increase. The fear of the girls has sent shockwaves through Mick and Bob who are looking everywhere and staying closer to you than before. James drops back slightly, and you notice him looking behind and to the left and right.

Then, from behind you all, there is an almighty CRAASSHHH in the wood as though three or four giant trees have fallen collectively. The almighty clattering sound reverberates around and sends your heart-rate through the roof. Everybody stops walking.

You stare at one another and fixe your gaze into the dense woodland.

Ushering everybody to lay down, you hide beneath the

long grass next to river and wait. A huge octopus-like tentacle whips through several trees severing off the thick branches and leaves, leaving only torn and ragged stumps. You stare intently as the others cower around you. Is it the same beast that had been in the cave?

No. This thunderous colossal being roars out from the thick woodland onto the open plains fifty feet from the river. It is pink, beige and faded yellow in colour; you can not see any feet and it only has one huge tentacle like a proboscis feeling around on the long grass in front. The body of this ginormous creature is long, elongated, shiny and slithery like a salamander. The weirdest thing about this slippery splattering species is the waving proboscis at the front of its long, lithe liquid-like body. One tentacle-type proboscis is at the front of its lythe body and another at its rear. They are identical, with one whipping and scanning the surface of the ground at the front, whilst another wriggles, squirms and whips around at the back.

The thickness of the beast's main body is double that of the single tentacles that swish and sway left and right at the front and back of its twenty feet long elongated body. You watch intently as it comes closer and closer. You realise that the actual vision of the creature must be poor as it relies on the touch of its tail and the senses from its single proboscis or antennae at the front. You whisper to the others: 'Stay here.'

You then run along the river bank and start splashing at the water from further up the stream. This immediately distracts the creature and it starts venturing towards where you are stood. You pick up a fallen branch and some big stones by the river bank. You begin to throw them into the water. Before you know it, this enormous, eerie, slippery critter wriggles fiercely in your direction and to your surprise leaps into the air from over a million spring-like miniature legs.

Airborne, you look at its underbelly to see your own reflection; your arm covers your face against the light reflecting from the mirror-silver surface of its belly. It lands in the shallows of the river you are trekking along. As it slithers and slopes along the side of the river, there is an almighty blast from behind it… BOOOOM! Almost as though an explosion has taken place in the water. As the spray and descending mist come down around you, you make out the sharp, silvery saw teeth of a massive fish head.

This new creature bursts through the water like a torpedo with its mouth as wide as a football goal and teeth bulging everywhere amongst its luminescent green gums. The jagged edges of each single tooth are clear, almost as though they have been highlighted black against the white silvery background of the enamel. The enormity of the fish head takes you aghast as it heads for the lythe beast on the river's edge.

You become transfixed with its bulging black eyes flickering with specks of gold. You only see half the fish's body out of the water and what you can make out are stripy gold and black lines set against a grey scaly skin. The circumference of the fish is eyewatering and in an instant it snaps down on the colossal salamander ripping its body in half. Bright yellow blood squelches out of its body and falls like acidic raindrops all around you.

As the blood lands it sputters and hisses, burning mini holes into the ground. You cover your head quickly.

Fortunately, you are only caught on your calf; a quick burning sensation evaporates within seconds. The giant fish detonates the water as it splashes back down from its catch. You are still in shock and disbelief and quickly make your way back to the group.

Bob is first to speak: 'What the hell was that?'

You are still catatonic and unable to speak. Mick looks at your shellshocked face. 'Are you OK, George?

You are fine, but your brain is still processing what you have just witnessed. 'Yeah, yeah, I'm fine.'

You reply is quiet as you are still awestruck by what you have seen. Hayley comes over to you and hugs you. Her warm body is comforting and helps straighten out your thoughts. James looks at you as Hayley envelops you in her arms. 'George, you've got to tell us what you saw, we could only make out noises and screeches from down in the grass. The girls were covering their ears it was so loud. As for Mick, his head was buried in the mud.'

Bob roars with laughter as Mick looks suitably disgruntled at James' remark. You note he doesn't contest James' comment, so you assume it to be true. The fear from the cave is back and the group cluster together to decide what to do. You need to show leadership and make a bold decision.

'We've got to carry on, staying here will only leave us as sitting targets. Going back into the cave is no refuge and our only hope of finding others still lies with this drinking water.'

For the rest of the afternoon you venture warily along the water's banks scanning left and right constantly. James stays at the back of the group whilst Mick and Bob walk with Hayley and Tracy. The long, wispy grass gives off an aromatic sweet smell like a freshly cut cucumber or cantaloupe melon. Your mind floats away to the thought of cutting into the crisp outer skin of a succulent cantaloupe melon, to enjoy the luscious juiciness within. This thought adjoins to the glowing sun, and warm wind fills you with contentment. Then you hear someone shout: 'George!'

James is calling you from the back of the group. It makes you jump as you are shaken from your delicious dream. James continues: 'George, what are we doing, can you not see the clouds ahead, it looks like a storm is brewing.'

You look up and notice the dark grey clouds swirling ominously ahead and looming down upon you. You think fast and make a decision that is going to upset the group: 'We're going in the woods.'

Bob is quick to retort: 'Are you mad? We don't know what's in there, after what happened this morning you want to go in there!'

Tracy echoes Bob's reservations: 'George, we've all had enough close calls. Don't you think it will be safer just to get wet.' You don't want to take the chance of being exposed but understand the reservations of the group. A rainstorm is approaching fast. You ask: 'Anyone else got a suggestion before we all get soaked for the night?' Tracy replies: 'What about up in the trees. They look huge and the branches seem to start quite low. Surely if we are off the ground that's a bit safer?

You think about Tracy's suggestion and it makes you immediately think back to the sizable salamander, slithering its slimy, mirrored torso towards you to suss out if you were for scoffing. You reply quickly to Tracy's proposal: 'Great

149

idea, Trace.'

And with that you jog towards the treeline around one hundred metres from the river bank. You call the others to come with you and they come over cautiously. You look up together at the giant trees around you and marvel at the speckled light which beams through the foliage onto the woodland floor. The beams of light feel holy in the mysterious, dense woodland around, which you know is dangerous.

Tracy catches the attention of the group: 'Look, there.'

She points at a huge tree, the enormity of which strikes you straight away. The circumference of the trunk is mammoth in size, you estimated it was at least 20metres around. It is by far the thickest, roundest, gnarliest and weirdly darkest tree you have ever seen.

There are nodules all around the base that could easily be used for stepping on and grabbing as you climb so you quickly scurry up around three metres from the floor. Next you hear Hayley: 'Be careful up there, we need you.'

It is a nice comforting gesture, but you need to explore, so venture further up the tree. The bark is so dark, it is like nothing you have ever seen before. Your mind recalls dark mahogany wood and you visualise a luxurious, distinguished brown colour, but this is much different, much darker. The bark borders on being black with hints of murky green and dusky brown. The blurry mossy spots tattoo the obscure surface which is difficult to focus upon because of its blackness. At around five metres high thick branches appear and you can tell they will easily hold your weight. You shout back down to the group. 'It's great up here. The branches are thick, its easy to climb and I reckon we'll be safe up here for the night. Not sure how we are going to sleep though; we need some material or flat wood to put between the branches.'

You can see the group below discussing what you have said. You are too high to listen though, so decide to climb a little further up the tree to see if you can make out the view beyond the canopy.

As you climb to around ten metres high you can see a tree hollow further above. You continue to climb and go above the hollow so that you can look down inside. The gaping gap in the bark is only discernible because of a thick, green moss like algae surrounding it. A giant oval shape of mouldy moss highlights this inner black circle of nothingness.

What has made this vast hole in the trunk? You peer inside and notice glutinous interior walls with tiny reflective droplets. As you reach inside to touch the interior of the tree you lose your footing on the branches of the tree and plummet headfirst inside the trunk. You yelp for help, but you are too far up the tree to be heard or even be seen, amongst the verdure of leaves and branches. The first thing you notice is that you haven't moved. Gravity would usually mean you fell, but the glutinous interior walls have clung to you like tar and you are suspended upside down inside the tree.

You can feel the blood pooling in your head as you hang suspended upside down. Try as you might, you can not move your body. Your clothes and your hands are stuck rigid and as you try to wriggle and squirm all that happens is a slow and gradual drop. You notice that you are descending ever so slightly. You are steadily and very, very, very slowly plunging deeper and deeper into the tree. Drip...... drip....... plop.......... plop.

Whatever substance you were stuck too is also falling around you and you can hear it as it lands. Plip... plop, and then you hear a noise that frightens you: pzzzzzzzzzsssssssssssssss BANG! A loud sizzle followed by a shuddering boom. You can't turn your head but gradually your nostrils begin to detect a rotten, eggy, gassy smell mixed with a vapour of gone-off fish. It is putrid, pure filth, and makes you immediately try to inhale, solely through your mouth.

The stench is unbearable and even a slight whiff makes you scrunch your face up and makes you want to be sick. You begin to realise you are heading hopelessly and possibly fatally towards a cauldron of toxic mulch. Slip... slip... drip... drop, you slide ever further into the tree and now it is clear, the distinct sound of bubbles bursting, popping, piercing your ear drums, and the sound reverberating around the inner base of tree trunk. Then, in a gap of silence you can make out a blood- curdling scream from the other side of the tree.

It is Hayley: 'Geeeeeoooooorrrrrggggggeeee!!'

It makes you think that the others have probably thought you have been attacked or something worse. They are part right, so you scream back at them: 'Hhhhhheeellllpppp!!!'

There is no response, but in your bat-like inverted state you focus deeply on the inner walls of the tree. You notice that the slimy interior continues to have flecks of light bouncing of the droplets. Where is this light coming from? You strain the sternocleidomastoid muscles in your neck to try, desperately, to look up. The hairs on the back of your head rip and your scalp bleeds as you strain every sinew to move your head just ten degrees forward.

As you peer back up the inside of the trunk, there, around twenty metres above your head, you can just make out the outline of a golden leaf. Glistening, floating near the top of the inside of the tree. You close your eyes and at the same time feel your head begin to burn. Your scalp is now dangerously close to the poisonous potash which spews and belches bubbles, bursting loudly by your ears, exploding droplets of acidic goo onto the top of your head. You have to move, you are going to die.

Chapter 13

'George, are you down there?' The deep, Latvian tones of Mikelis fill your heart with joy and your mind with hope. You shout back: 'Mick, Mick, hurry. I'm burning!' Mick's head is looking down into the hollow of the tree and you shout up to him, 'Mick, look up. If you can grab beyond that leaf you'll clasp a bee. The bee will light up this hollow.'

With your instruction, Mick tentatively puts his size fourteen feet on the edge of the mossy ridge and carefully, delicately eases his frame into the hollow. He is in the shape of an italic capital I. You shout instructions: 'Don't touch the sides Mick, whatever you do, don't touch the sides. Place both arms above your head together like you are a long thin sausage.'

Mick chortles: 'Not sure about the thin, but I know what you mean.'

Mick has a huge frame and is quite bulky. You can only just make out the outline of this eighteen stone man. He is looking like he is on the top board of a diving platform ready to plunge into a pool. Mick asks nervously: 'Now what?'

You can tell he is teetering on the edge of the hollow and rocking dangerously back and forth with his forehead dangerously close to attaching itself to the tacky adhesive internal walls of the tree. You shout up: 'You have got to jump up, Mick. Grab that leaf and there will be a bee on top of it.

Once you're holding the bee, I guarantee there'll be light inside this tree.'

Mick looks up at the golden glowing leaf radiating a murky luminosity. The glow sheds speckled glimpses of light all around. Before jumping, Mick crouches a little in preparation to explode vertically up towards the leaf. As he presses down during his take off, Mick's giant feet break part of the mossy, hollow ridge he has been balancing on. Mick loses his footing as he jumps and flails desperately in mid air, swiping at the golden leaf. It disintegrates into a million minute pieces, so small they could not be seen.

To Mick, it appears that the leaf has evaporated instantaneously. In a blind panic, he snatches at the leaf. Mick then begins to fall. Instead of sticking to the sides of the internal wall like you, Mick just falls like a dead weight.

Not in a straight line though, oh no. As he falls, Mick bumps and bounces, turns and twists as he collides with the interior of the tree. You feel the wooden shell of the tree reverberate and shudder as Mick comes crashing down, coming to an abrupt halt next to you. His horrible, hairy, sweaty belly smearing against your upside-down face.

Mick lands with his feet firmly planted in the gunk and you immediately fear for his life and his legs! 'Mick, are you all right?'

He is a little shaken, but replies straight away: 'Phew, that was a bit crazy. My foot slipped but as soon as I grabbed at the leaf my hand began to vibrate and as I fell it was like I was in a dream. It was like falling in slow motion on a bouncy castle; as I hit the sides and spiralled out of control, it was almost joyful. No pain, just spongey fun.'

In a dreaded alarm, you start to shout at him: 'Mick, Mick, Mick, your legs, are they burning?'

He chuckles in his deep, Latvian tenor voice as you feel his lips talking at your belly. 'What are you on about George, this stuff is like a warm slush puppy, it smells delicious too. Do you reckon I could eat it?'

You are confused. Moments before Mick had entered the tree you were in fear of your life. You couldn't inhale through your nose, your head felt like it was on fire and you had strained every muscle in your neck to wrench your head from the extreme, gummy resin that attached you upside down to the inside of the tree.

As this thought come to you, you feel your achilles tendons peeling away simultaneously from the tree, in unison with your calves, hamstrings and bum. In a flash your back detaches too and you drop head first into the gooey gunk that Mick is already stood in. Mick howls with laughter. You wave your arms around frantically trying to push your way back to the surface and then you feel two giant hands grab you from underneath your armpits and pull you to the surface.

After Mick lifts you out of the gunge you both stand there looking down at the knee deep, vibrant, yellow slime. It then dawns on you that you can see the liquid mess and that the whole interior of the tree is glowing in a yellowy hue. You look at Mick and say: 'Are you still holding that bee? To which Mick replies: 'What bee?'

You look at Mick and roll your eyes in an exasperated manner, 'Remember….. I told you to grab the bee on top of the golden leaf?'

Mick looks in his right hand and there it is, lying

motionless and looking squashed and crumpled. One of the bee's wings begins to flutter and then, as its body turns, both wings begin to flutter.

The golden yellowy hue inside the tree gets brighter and brighter. The sweet fragrant sugary smell of the liquid you are stood in gets stronger and stronger. Mick looks bemused as he stares at the bee and then looks around: 'What is this?'

Mick is discombobulated by the entire episode of events and you can see why, but first you want to taste the stuff you are stood in as it smells amazing. You bend down and cup the liquid with both hands; raising it above your mouth, it drips slowly down.

The intoxicating, syrupy goodness sends quivers down your spine, as the smooth flow of this sumptuous, molten fluid delivers a warm, flavoursome hit to your mouth. You feel every drop run down your throat, coating your oesophagus and warmly lining your stomach. It is pure ecstasy. You turn to Mick: 'Try eating some of that, it's from another planet.'

Mick hands you the trembling bee so that he can bend down to scoop up some of the golden goodness he is standing in. As he transfers the bee from his hands to yours, the light inside the tree flickers momentarily. From his knelt position, Mick looks up at you. You answer him without him talking: 'It's fine Mick, everything is fine.'

The big, burly brute puts his shovel like hands into the gooey goodness and you watch as his face comes alive as he smiles gleefully. Mick looks at you: 'Wow, that is some good stuff.' He promptly cups another load of the rich, syrupy slop and sucks it out of his huge palms.

You marvel at your new surroundings: the dark dingy cold tree is gone and now you stand inside a glowing, radiant cavern of sheer happiness and joy. The dangerous, dripping acidic resin was now edible and has changed from a dark green black sludge to a chewy gooey treacle.

You think about the others outside and can make out the screams of Tracy and Hayley against the contrasting bellows of Bob and James. They are calling for you both and have no way of knowing you are deep inside the gut of the tree. Mick turns to you with the golden molasses dripping from his chin and smeared around his face. He speaks: 'If we can hear them, George, then surely, they can hear us?'

You turn to him, smiling in your mind at the childish mess he has made of his face. You bow your head solemnly and speak towards the floor, 'Mick, you didn't hear my screams earlier, no-one did. What makes you think they will hear us now?'

Mick grabs you hard by the shoulders and this makes you look up immediately and stop feeling sorry for yourself. He says directly: 'Look around you, George, this is not the same place you fell into. The walls are different, the light is different, even the feeling in here is different. I'm telling you, George, I bet the acoustics have changed as well.'

It makes you think Mick is right. What are you waiting for? You roar: 'Bob, can you hear me!'

You wait…. 'George, is that you?'

With a huge smile, you look at Mick and then holler back: 'Bob, we're in the bottom of the tree. I know that might sound weird but we both fell in here.'

You can hear Tracy and Hayley crying tears of joy and

James then speaks in his dulcet tones: 'How have you both ended up inside a tree?

You are relieved to hear all of their voices and reply:

'Look guys, it's a long story, but we need to think of a way to get out. There's no way Mick and me can get back to where we fell in so you'll have to think of some way to get us out.'

Mick then speaks: 'What about that vine-type rope we used when we entered the cave at the top, or any large pieces of wood we could wedge in here and build some sort of crude ladder to climb out.' You like what Mick is saying: 'That's a great idea. If any of you could climb up the tree, you'll see the hollow we came through.'

For a few seconds there is silence and then you can hear James talking to the other three. The next noise you hear is a huge cracking sound and then you realise they are snapping branches to help you get out. Bob is moaning, as usual, about them being too big as the ladies enthusiastically pull down nearby branches whilst on the shoulders of James. At one point, you hear Tracy fall to the cackle of laughter from Hayley and James; your initial fear relaxes and you stop pressing your ear to the tree. Mick looks over to you: 'Mate, you need to relax.'

You can see his point of view, as there is little else you can do, so you decide to slouch back and relax in the bubbling, beautiful basin you are already stood in.

Sitting down in the warm, sweet, effervescing liquid, your nostrils are filled with its sweet aroma. Your tense muscles begin to relax and you close your eyes as the sensual, sizzling slush swirls around your body leaving you in a deep relaxing trance. As you lay there you open one eye and look at the bee in your hand. It is time to tell the others everything about your past.

Chapter 14

As you peer up you can see the outline of James' black hand against the gleaming yellow walls of the inside of the tree. You shout up to him: 'James, we're down here, just be care...'

Before you can finish your sentence, James' whole body comes tumbling through the outside layer of the tree. Unbeknown to you, the hole you had come through was broken and rotting. The ridge where Mick's foot had previously slipped crumbles around James' gripped hands and big chunks of the bark break loose. You cover your head as the debris rains down inside and James falls awkwardly towards you, shouting as he falls, 'Aaaahhhhhhhhhh!'

Just like Mick before, he bounces off the interior walls and then splllaaasshhh, he belly-flops, spread like a starfish into the warm sweet liquid you have been bathing in.

Mick wades towards him and you quickly follow. 'James, James, are you OK?' As he lifts his face from the soppy liquid his eyes are wide open. He looks round at you and starts to smile. Then Mick starts to laugh and the three of you are soon in hysterics, splashing around and laughing in the gilded treacle.

As you all calm down, you are all still smiling and soon you can hear Hayley and Tracy shouting out James' name. They are yelling: 'James, James, can you hear us up there, are you OK? We heard something crack, are you still up there?'

James replies in his deep voice: 'Tracy, I'm fine. Thank-you for caring. I fell into the tree with the other two, but we're all here and we're all OK. You should come and join us, it's lovely and warm in here.'

You hadn't realised it was cold outside, but you are a bit wary of Tracy and Hayley coming into the tree. The whole point of Mick and James coming to find you was to get you out. You voice your thoughts: 'Hold on a minute, girls. Before you come in here we need to think of a way to get out.'

You hear Bob shout back: 'My thoughts exactly, but you're too late!' The girls excitedly pop their heads through the gap in the tree which is now significantly larger than when you had first slipped through. Tracy's chin rests on top of Hayley's head as they are giggling and laughing, looking down at you all sat in the warm, bubbling, edible jacuzzi.

Tracy shouts down: 'We're coming in.' And with that, Hayley climbs over her head and shoots down one side of the inside of the tree like a water flume. As she lands, she causes an almighty splash as her feet strike the oozing, yellowy goop. She shouts up the tree to Tracy: 'Trace, you've got to get in here, it's so warm and just smells amazing.'

Fortunately, Tracy has taken heed of Bob's warning and shouts down to the group: 'I don't want to leave Bob. We've got to work out how to make that hole even bigger so we can climb in and you can climb out.' Tracy then climbs back down the tree to join Bob. The sun is starting to go down and it will soon be dark.

You think about the bee and how it might be able to help but realise this would show the group the power it held. What are you thinking? They already knew your stories of the bee so it is time to show them. In your mind you want the bee to act as a cut, a type of blade or axe. You have witnessed the bees act in unison before like a giant laser cutting into the Earth's crust. You shout to Bob: 'Right, listen Bob, I'm going to send you a bee. You need to find a sturdy stick and the bee will act as its head, like that of an axe or a hammer.'

Bob shouts back, 'Are you smoking wacky-backy in there?'

Mick replies: 'Listen, Bob, I can vouch for George on this one. The tree looked dead when I climbed up and looked inside. It was dark, dirty, lifeless and rotten. George told me to grab the bee and when I did there was a miraculous change, a life affirming change. You've got to trust us, Bob, I believed in George and you've got to believe in the power of this bee.'

You hope Mick's persuasion and impassioned speech will hold more sway with Bob and you let go of the bee. Mick turns to you: 'How does it know where to go?'

You reply: 'Because I've told it.'

Mick, James and Tracy look at you in confusion. James remarks: 'So, you're a bee whisperer now?'

You want to tell them everything but wait for Bob. The next thing you hear is an excitable Tracy: 'George, it's come, the bee has come.' It comes down like one of those fireflies glowing in the dark. You know of the bioluminescence that the bee possesses and are pleased the others can finally witness it with their own eyes.

Bob shouts: 'I can't believe it, the thing is sat on top of my stick. What should I do?'

There is a pause as you think about hurting the bee, but you realise its incredible power and reply: 'Swing you stick like an axe, Bob. Hit the tree.' The next sound you hear is,

THWACK, THWACK, CRACK against the outside bark of the tree. Then a pause. You feel really dizzy and James leans over to you and puts his hand and on your shoulder. 'Are you OK, George?'

You hold your face in both hands to try and regain some composure. Tracy is shouting through the tree and the light emanating around you begins to flicker and fade. James, who is licking his fingers winces: 'Eeeerggghh, this honey's turned sour.'

A lightbulb switches on in your head. That was it, you have been bathing in the honey of the bees. Their wellbeing is represented in this tree. When the bees are happy, content and at ease the tree will reflect this. The yellow hue, the warm honey, the sweet sugary taste. The reverse also appears to be true; if the bees are unhappy, their environment quickly turns. Mick rolls his head and says to you: 'Is it me, or is it getting cold in here?'

You realise that Bob and Tracy have unknowingly knocked the poor bee unconscious. This was under your direction and you feel incredibly guilty. You shout to Tracy: 'Tracy, take the bee from the stick and cup it in your hands. Blow on it ever so gently.' Your advice is intuitive, and you pray for it to work.

It is not long before the dull, eery surroundings inside the tree begin to brighten and Tracy shouts through to you: 'It's starting to glow again. The bee, it's glowing.'

You reply: 'OK, this time place the bee on top of the stick and reach up as far as you can on the tree. I'm going to place my hand the other side.'

Tracy's excitement grows: 'George, the stick, the whole

stick is bright white, it's glowing just like the bee.'

You had an inkling the bee would feel your energy and come to you. So you usher Mick towards you and tell him to put you on his giant shoulders. You then instruct James to support Mick, but also to hold your ankles steady as your whole body lifts onto Mick's shoulders.

You place both palms just below the gaping hole. Hayley shouts to her friend: 'Tracy, can you hear me?'

She replies: 'Yes.'

You want Bob to ensure her safety, so you reply, 'Tracy, I want you to climb up a few notches on the tree with the stick in your hand and the bee on top. Trust me. Bob, just be Tracy's safety net.'

He replies: 'No probs, we've got this.'

You can make out the feint sound of Tracy scratching and pulling herself up the outside of the tree. You get Mick and James in position and climb up upon Mick's shoulders. 'OK, Tracy, now place the stick just below the gap where Hayley came into the tree earlier.'

You place your palms flat on the inside of the tree and feel a warm emanating heat. You lean forward and place your forehead just underneath your outstretched hands, pressing against the inside walls of the tree. You close your eyes and silently implore the bee to start cutting into the outside bark. The next noise you hear is a high-pitch shrill...... it isn't the bee, it is Tracy. 'Look, look Bob, look!'

Bob, who is acting as Tracy's safety net can't really see what is going on. You hear him say, 'What is it, Tracy? I can't see.'

She replies: 'The bee looks like it's gnawing through the wood. Like the tip of a hot knife, the whole stick is slicing slowly through the bark so easily. It is like a white-hot laser just zapping the wood and burning right through.'

As she speaks you shout to Tracy, 'Just keep it steady, Tracy.'

The bee is coming to you and gradually you hear a drill-type sound coming towards your head, so you back off from the inside of the tree.

The bee suddenly bursts through and hits you between the eyes. The shock of it causes you to lurch back and fall back down. Mick loses his balance and as you fall James, who was holding your ankles, falls backwards too. It wis like a circus act that has gone wrong as all three of you fall backwards into the viscous fluid below. The bee follows you as you fall, glowing all the time and sending rays of flashing light around the now dingy tree. You expect to splash as you land on your back, but instead you are cushioned onto a spongey airbed. Hayley is sat there, looking at the three of you: 'What the hell is going on? As you lot fell I screamed, but nothing came out of my mouth. The next I knew I was sitting cross legged on this huge, puffy, hexagonal cushion.'

You look around and the previously yellowy slush has solidified and turned into a bouncy, spongey hexagonal jigsaw. There are hundreds, if not thousands of different sized hexagonal, encrusted, prismatic, pillowy cells and inside the boundaries of each hexagon is a slightly raised puffy cushion. It hits you like a sledgehammer and you blurt out spontaneously, 'This is their honey!'

Your final syllable falls away to the sound of a huge whirring propeller. A continuous buzzing noise as though a jumbo jet is getting ready to take off. You can just make out Bob's voice through the din: 'Watch out in there, it's a swarm, looks like thousands of them, watch out.'

Before you know it a huge cloud of bees gather above you and the others and heading directly towards you all. The four of you cower down, holding your knees to your chests and tucking your heads in.

They land everywhere and the place begins to tremble with their vociferous vibrations. You check on everyone and shout above the din: 'Is everyone OK?' You do not hear a response so shout again: 'Is everyone OK?'

You see a slim, long human body covered head to toe in bees put a thumb in the air: at least James was coping. You look behind you and Mick is writhing around scratching and shooing the bees from his muscular body, but they irritably keep returning. You gather he is OK though because he isn't screaming. Hayley is huddled in a ball and the bees have made her look like a fluffy, vibrating, yellow and black Christmas bauble. You can just make out her piercing blue eyes through the thousands of bees and by looking at those eyes you know she is OK.

You think to check on Bob and Tracy outside. 'Bob, can you hear me?' Your voice is slightly muffled as bees crawl across your lips and nostrils. He replies, 'I'm fine, but is Tracy in there with you? She's not up the tree anymore?'

You frantically look around. Had she fallen in as the white beam sliced through the wood? You wouldn't know as the swarm of bees had buried you into the cushioned honeycomb you are now softly and slowly bouncing upon. You scan the inside of the tree and spot a long object covered in bees. It is both the stick and the outstretched arm of Tracy sliding slowly half way down the viscous honey walls. You crawl over towards her feet and call up to her: 'Tracy, can you hear me, are you OK?'

You can tell she is still stunned as her arm remains outstretched and looks a little odd with her collapsed body leaning on the inside of the tree, surrounded by buzzing, rambling, exploratory bees. She looks down at you to speak: 'George, is that you?'

You reply, 'Yes, Tracy, are you OK?'

Her rigid arm slumps to the floor as she answers: 'Well, I'm in here now I guess we're all doomed and it's all my fault?'

You are quick to respond: 'Stop it, Tracy, none of this is your fault, you've been brilliant, and you shouldn't be so down on yourself.'

You have been through a lot with Tracy and your affection towards her has grown. There was no love at first sight, but with time you have warmed to one another as you have shared experiences which have brought you closer together.

You ask for her opinion: 'What do you think about Bob out there? Shall we encourage him to come inside, it must be getting dark?'

Tracy is quite practical and replies, 'Well, I reckon if you could get on James' shoulders you could reach that gap, so that means, potentially, we could always get out. So yeah, get him in here for the night; at least it'll be warmer and he'll be with us, but he'll moan about the noise!'

Tracy is of course referring to the incessant buzzing of the thousands of bees that are scattered everywhere, covering you all like gold and black pimples. They aren't stinging and you feel relatively safe, so you call Bob into your lair.

'Bob, can you hear me?'

He calls back: 'Yes, is Tracy in there?'

You reassure his nervous voice: 'Yes, she's fine. In fact she misses you.' You laugh and then ask: 'Bob, why don't you come in here. The bees are very friendly and I promise they won't sting. Come on in and join us.'

Bob, unsurprisingly, questions your logic: 'But how are we all going to get out if I come in?'

You use Tracy's suggestion as an example: 'It's fine, I can stand on James' shoulders and be able to reach the gap to get out in the morning. Now, come on in here, it's warm and the conversation is better than out there!'

You hear Bob chuckle as he replies, 'I'm not sure about that last bit, but it is getting cold so I'm coming up.'

Bob climbs up the outside of the tree and pops his head in the gap that had been made bigger by Tracy's incision with the glowing light stick. The golden hue from inside the tree is emanating out of the hole into the darkness and you can just make out flies and other small creatures dashing across the golden rays in the darkness of the night. Bob asks: 'Now what? How do I get down there?'

He is peering down what appears to be about a ten metre drop. Hayley unravels herself from her foetal ball position and calls to him: 'Bob, when you land it's like a trampoline. You'll be fine.'

You think Bob might require more cajoling and encouragement, but Hayley's soft and tender tones appear to do the trick. He leaps ungainly into the tree and lands with a thud. As he approaches the soft hexagonal matrix below, the bees part swiftly and his giant rear plants in the largest, centre hexagon of the whole golden template. Although his landing is cushioned, there is a reactive force which rebounds him into the air. He twists and shouts: 'Whhooooooaahhhhh.'

Before face planting next to Mick. Everyone laughs, including Bob. You feel relief. Everyone is safe... or so you think.

Chapter 15

It is hard to sleep that night: you feel hot and uncomfortable. Restless and agitated you move from side to side and rolled about on the uneven hexagons that are raised a little like domed cushions. Their soft fuzzy surface feels like an uneven airbed and the constant buzz of the bees around your face and ears becomes ever so annoying.

Mick, on the other hand, is out for the count. Slumped against the inside of the tree his snores are so loud it feels like the tree shakes every time he inhales. James is coiled serenely next to Tracy and Hayley who were hugging each other in a spooned position. You can tell Bob is a light sleeper like you, as he is rolling around trying to brush off the bees, like Mick had been doing an hour or so before him. The hazy light also doesn't help, but at least it makes you feel safe as you can see your surroundings.

As the night gets colder the bees around you start to gather in thick clusters and start to move around the tree space as big spheres. There are around thirty of these beach-ball-size spheres delicately bobbing around the hexagonal cushions. You watch on in amazement as everyone else is in a deep sleep. It soon becomes icy cold and you wish you could cover the hole above your head where a bitter breeze rushes in and brushes the insides of the tree and circulates the air around you.

As you shiver, you notice the dark, yellowy-brown lines

that give the outline to each hexagon thicken and then start to rise. Like cakes in an oven they pop up from around each hexagonal cushion to form definite hard blocks of….. gold. They are gold, solid bars of gold. You can't believe your eyes as more and more of these heavy blocks emerge from the edges of the prismatic, pillowy cells. The others had unknowingly moved closer to one another during the night and soon you can hear grunting and moaning as they are poked and prodded by the gold bars rising from below them. The first to wake is Hayley.

She scratches at her puffy, red eyes and then exclaims,

'Am I dreaming or am I surrounded by a load of gold bars? What the hell is happening?'

You look at her with a huge smile on your face and reply:

'I know. Crazy, right?'

The both of you stare as more and more solid gold emerges around the inside perimeter of the tree and then starts to spread like veins into the myriad of hexagonal prisms around you.

The gold glistens and shines and sparkles and makes you feel rich. It draws you in, absorbs you and makes you lose your mind in a fantasy world of fast cars, big houses, designer clothes and private jets. Then you recognise the paradoxical predicament you are in.

Who wants gold? What does gold represent? You only know six people and all they want is food and shelter. Gold is pointless. Gradually, the others start to wake up and marvel at what is around them. Bob tries to pick up a block but it does not move. Mick is next and, before you know it, everyone is yanking and tugging and trying their hardest to lift these solid gold blocks from between the velvety cushioned hexagons.

You watch in amazement and then notice James looking at you: 'Why aren't you trying?'

You looked at him and reply: 'James, I thought you had more about you. What are you going to do with a bar of gold?'

He doesn't reply and stands there, a little dumbfounded, so you continue: 'Are you going to cash it in at the bank? Err, oh, that's right, there are no banks. But it's OK, you could trade it for a car......... whoops, no cars and no roads. I know, what about a yacht or even better a plane to get us out of here?'

Your voice has got louder and louder and the others are now looking at you. James speaks: 'OK, OK, I get your point, but come on, when have you ever seen this much gold?'

You give a succinct response: 'Right now, if I offered to break off one of these gold bars and give you a block, or offer you a roasted hog, what would you take?'

Mick cuts across James: 'Hog all day, I'm starving!'

You look at everyone: 'Exactly. Let's think logically, people. We all know what gold used to be, but we are in a different world now and its only real use would be if we could build something with it, kill something to eat or reflect the sunlight to heat something. Oh, I don't know. What's the point?'

You throw your hands in the air, exasperated and annoyed. You slump back to the floor. As your bum hits the soft, furry surface of the hexagonal cushions beneath you there is a cold and uncomfortable feeling. Ttthhwaaaanngggggg, pop, BANG... BANG... BANG !!!!

It is as though kinks in a metal sheet are being flattened. You look around at the once furry, soft, cushioned domes as they began to straighten flat and turn into solid metal sheets of gold. The bees buzz furiously around, falling quickly from their spheres and dropping onto these newly formed golden sheets. It is like bullets hitting the tin signs in a cowboy western movie. Ping..... ping..... like tiny specks of metallic rain falling from a bee cloud. The bees bounce like fleas and boing around on the glossy, glittery, metal sheets.

Thousands of them appearing to have frivolous fun as they fall from their spheres. Pinging off the polished golden sheets their wings are loose with their little legs flailing and their chubby round bodies floppy and rolling around. You are sure you could make out tiny miniscule smiles on their faces at what appear to be unbridled joy and a release of pleasure.

Their antennae droop back and forth, and their little heads roll from side to side. They rebound off one another in the air and that just seems to make them more joyous and playful. You'd never envisaged seeing bees like this.

The group is aghast and watch with glee as the bees frolic and flip around in a crazy, Amazonian tribal dance. You watch intently and start to notice that although the bees seem to randomly spring from one metal plate to another, none are touching the biggest and most central metal plate. They are going over it, to the side of it and some even momentarily come out of their trance-like state to avoid landing on it and flutter quickly to an adjacent hexagon.

You whisper what you were witnessing to Bob who is closest to you on your right shoulder. He passes the message on and the whole group start nodding at each other and everyone is a little perplexed.

You can not resist finding out what is so special about the central hexagon and curiosity gets the better of you. As you approach the centre you stand there, and nothing. You crouch down to touch the metal sheet, and nothing, neither hot, nor cold. You usher the others over. The six of you are tightly packed on this one hexagon and the bees start to avoid all of you.

Tracy speaks up: 'Err what are we actually doing?'

You reply: 'I don't really know, but at least we know where to stand if we don't want the bees climbing all over us.'

Bob laughs: 'I wouldn't worry, they seem happy enough to me. I think they could be drunk!'

Mick quips: 'I want some of whatever they've been drinking.'

Then it strikes you. The bees have swarmed back to their honeycomb inside the tree and now that it has solidified they are showing off to one another. These are all male bees and you are guessing the queen bee, the prized bee, may be waiting beyond the central hexagon.

You turn to the others and in the time it takes to swivel your head up from looking at the floor, it has disappeared from beneath you. All of you vanish and as you shoot down, what appears to be some sort of flume, you scream at Tracy: 'Have you got the stick, Tracy?'

She holds up her arm and a huge sense of relief radiates through your veins. You shout: 'Let me hold it.'

You put it in your hands, close your eyes and focus.

As the golden glow of the bees above you begins to fade, a single white dot starts to accelerate towards you as you fall helplessly into the pitch-black abyss. The others are screaming and shouting, frightened for their lives. You remain calm and narrow your focus on the white speck which is travelling faster and faster towards you. It now feels like you have been falling for an age; death is a certainty upon impact. Then the bee, glowing like a firefly, lands atop the stick and the whole thing glows like a fluorescent torch.

Like a Halloween sparkler you swirl it around three hundred and sixty degrees and count-off the group. You see James, Tracy and Hayley, then further below you, Mick, and further still Bob.

You continue to descend but the rays of light emanating from the stick do not show a floor nor any walls around you. This is it, your time has come and you feel annoyed that you have still not spoken about the truth with these people who you trusted with your life.

Your luminescent wand reminds you of an airport traffic controller waving a plane in from the tarmac in the dark. This time, though, there is no plane and you are helplessly waving the stick around to find something, anything, to give you hope. You are giving up rapidly when unexpectedly your wavering wand catches the reflection of some sort of glass or translucent plastic.

You quickly wave the light around and notice you are in some sort of funnel which is getting narrower and narrower. Mick and Bob, who are ahead of you, begin to clatter the sides and you shout down to them: 'Mick, Bob, stay straight, put your legs together and arms by your side.'

You do not want them to break any limbs nor injure themselves. After you call to them you look and notice they have followed your instruction and within a split second they are wedged back to back with their rotund bellies squished against the see-through glass or plastic. You quickly shout, 'Watch out!!!' Followed by, 'Cover your head!'

Tracy and Hayley rattle onto the top of Mick and Bob and as they do Mick and Bob disappear. Tracy and Hayley have taken their place wedged in the narrow pipe part of the funnel and have pushed them down beyond your sight. You can see that you and James are going to crash into them imminently and scream at them, but you are too late. As you hurtle into the two ladies, all four of you scream together: 'Aaaahhhh!'

James and you have come to an abrupt halt. You are kissing James. Not intentionally: your lips are touching because you have ended up face-to-face in the narrow part of the funnel and your hips and bum are stuck, leaving your legs dangling below in what feels like space.

Your force and speed as you plummeted has pushed Tracy and Hayley out and the next thing you feel are hands pulling on your dangling legs, feet and ankles. You can make out the voices of the four below you, as they shout: 'It's OK, we're all alive and we're pulling you out.'

Plop! You fall onto a dark red, almost purple, regal tick carpeted floor. You look around and the place looks familiar, but you can't recall it immediately. This is getting strange and you think it is about time you tell the truth.

'Right, everyone, I want you to sit at that long table over there.' A table? Chairs? Where the hell are you? Everyone pulls out a chair from the long, antique table and sits down. You take a deep breath and begin from the start: 'One day I was going into work and everything was normal when I received this letter.'

You pause for breath and the group reply in robotic unison: 'We know.'

You shake your head: 'No, no, no, you don't understand, these two 'agents' turned up, they turned my colleague's head into a zebra.' You stutter and repeat your words as you continue to tell your story: 'And, and, and they attacked my other colleague with crabs. I mean, crabs! Who does that? It was madness, the whole thing was complete madness and the next thing I know I'm in a pit of snakes.'

You pause again, look around at everyone waiting for some sort of shock on their faces or bewilderment at the story you are telling. Instead they all replied in unison again: 'We know, George.'

You are angry. Are they not listening to your stories about the zebras, the crabs, the snakes? It was sheer craziness. As you continue your story it dawns on you: 'When I was in this pool of snakes, I was dragged out and...'

They all cut into your sentence, 'We know, George.'

By now you are getting annoyed and suspect something is going on within the group. 'Go on then, go on, tell me what happened next. I dare you.'

There is silence. You could hear a pin drop as they all look at each other from around the table and shrug their shoulders. You finally feel as though you are being listened to. 'OK, now this might sound a bit far fetched and what I am about to tell you may make you hate me, but I promise I did it for our planet, for the love of our planet. Now remember, I had family too, you know. I was married for goodness sake!'

Tracy stops your rant: 'It's OK, George, we're listening.'

As you start to repeat your story about the maid and your journey, Bob stops you. 'George, we love you, but can you give us the short version please.'

You know they are not interested and probably won't believe you anyhow. 'OK, so, basically, I got bees, special golden bees, powerful bees, to lift every piece of solid land on our planet as we know it and turn every land mass onto its side.'

You pause and look around. No-one reacts, so you continue: 'After all the land had been turned, I'm not really sure what happened to me. I just remember being at one, feeling peace, really appreciating every aspect of our world and then from nowhere I was with you guys by a campfire.'

You look towards Bob as you know he has always been suspicious of you. He looks straight back at you: 'It's OK, George, I know.'

You go mad: 'Know! You know, do you? Stop saying you bloody know. None of you know what I've been through, what I've done and how we've ended up here.'

The other five stand up together and you feel a little insecure as, at first, they looked at one another, before fixing their gaze on you. Together they say: 'George, we've been there with you, from the beginning.'

James then speaks: 'Your office, George. I was the agent.'

Tracy then speaks: 'And so was I.'

Bob and Mick then add to the reveal. Mick is first. 'When you came to the villa, this villa in fact, I was the guy who dragged you from the snake pit and gave you to James.'

As Mick is speaking your brain begins to spin. You looked

at him and remember the big brute of a man, an East European thug who had dragged you from the pool of snakes. Could it have been Mick? James is next to speak. He calmly explains: 'Mick brought you to me, George, remember I was wearing a tailored suit, tasselled shoes and it wasn't long before I was floating above your face. I don't think you liked me too much back then George, as you took a swipe at me.'

James starts to laugh, and Mick copies him with a sly cackle. You aren't impressed. These people have kidnapped you, threatened you and tortured you and now they are laughing at you. This isn't right, so you slam your hands on the table to stop them from laughing and gain their complete attention.

'Hold up, you're telling me that you knocked me out, took me to your lair, dragged me to that room, and mentally and physically tortured me. What part of that is funny, exactly what part?'

You pause waiting for a reaction, and they all look at the table solemnly. Bob then says, meekly: 'I did save you from the snake bites though, George. I was the doctor, remember?'

Bob's humble admission does not cut much ice with you and you are still seething. He then continues: 'We came to you, George. Mick and me morphed and we came to you.'

You stop him: 'Morphed?'

Bob and Mick look at you, then look at each other. They both climb onto the table and walk towards each other. Bob and Mick touch foreheads and place their palms against each other. Their bodies start to coagulate and reform and, in a whirl of wispy gold and shredded buttery light, they become one.

On the table a giant of a man unfurls himself: he is huge, muscular and looks immense. You stare for a while in amazement, not because of what you have just witnessed, but because it is him. The man in front of you now has bowed in front of you before. The man looks up at you with his bony brow and thick Neanderthal skull: 'Emperor, you are the ruler of gold, the controller, you govern the land, the sea and the sky. You have released us and we come with you, we follow you, you are our leader.'

You notice the others around the table have dropped to the floor and are all bowed on one knee. You go back over everything in your mind and without noticing you start to talk aloud: 'So, James and Tracy are the agents, Mick is the bully, James is the distinguished one, Bob is the doctor. Bob and Mick, well, you're just, well, you know......'

You stop to marvel at the enormous man now bowed on one knee in front of you on the long antique wooden table. You hastily shout: 'Aha, so Hayley, you must be the maid?'

Hayley looks up at you from the floor: 'No, sir, that was not me.'

You reply: 'Then who was that and who are you?'

Hayley enlightens you: 'The maid is our queen, sir. In fact, I am her maid. She sent me here with the others to be sure she had chosen wisely, to be sure you are the doctor, the Emperor and our new leader. Sir, you are the ruler of gold.'

You ask Hayley: 'Why do you call me a doctor? You called me that when you came for me in my office?

She replies: 'You hold mercurial governance over the bees and they are the gold. You are the controller of gold, you shape the gold, you are the doctor, the Emperor and our leader.'

You ask the question you had asked so many times before: 'But why me?'

Tracy starts: 'George, you have shown courage, fearlessness in the face of danger and consideration of others before yourself.'

Hayley adds: 'You have sought safety, food and shelter for all of us. Always thinking of our wellbeing before your own.'

Bob continues: 'You have created plans and followed through on what you have said. You have listened to other people's opinions and accepted the views of others; even in the face of hostility you have shown compassion and care. You have taken on board suggestions and integrated them into your own plans, and have never turned your back on the thoughts of others. You have shown us conviction, courage and direction in times of despair. You have embraced our differences.'

Mick took up the conversation when Bob had finished: 'You have shown bravery, camaraderie and valour in the face of danger. You have listened, deeply listened, to those around you, you have faced adversity head on and never shied away from the challenges that lie before you.'

James completed the group's tribute towards you: 'You have been a friend to us all but, importantly, you have led us. George, please take heed of what we have said. You are the one: the controller, the Emperor, our leader.'

You sit in silence, taking in what had just been said. The journey to this point has been intuitive, it has been from your heart. You have made some big decisions and then followed up those decisions with decisive action. You have never wavered, you have never second guessed; you have listened, considered, but always moved forward. Perhaps they are right, perhaps it is time to lead. To lead what?

James looks at you and says solemnly: 'George, you must recognise that this has been a test. Our great queen came to you in a time of need and wanted to test your commitment and devotion to a new world. Your old world had become soiled with deceit, hatred, pollution, greed and selfishness. Your old world needed turning over like the soil of a farmer's field. It will come back, George, but needs time to find itself again. The bottom of the oceans have been exposed to air for the first time and this will bring new life, new flora and fauna which will thrive and evolve with time. The world needs to be taken over again by nature. You will return, George, but for now you must come and lead us.'

You look back at James: 'But where?'

You are confused and trying to make sense of what James and the others have said. James replies to you: 'You are coming with us, my friend, my leader. You are leaving this planet to come with us.'

As James speaks he pushes back away from the table. The others follow him one at a time. Bob, Tracy, Mick and Hayley. The long dark antique table then rises slowly from the ground and hangs suspended in the air. The chairs quickly follow and then you hear a high-pitch, squealing, joyful, happy sound shrieking towards you.

As you look up at the table now dangling freely, two purple ethereal wafts of air appear and came hurtling down, skidding and bouncing off the vertical table. Hopping and bounding from table to chair, across and over and under until landing on each of your shoulders:

'Hello there, George old son, it's Rose and Dandelion here. We thought we might help you at this particular point in time before you leave us for good.'

The fairies. You have seen them twice before. Once with the maid under the tree and once in the belly of the beast from the cave. You trust them, they have been your guiding light. Right, now you really wanted some guidance, some pertinent advice to help you in this very confusing situation. Rose is first to speak: 'Be true to your heart dear George, you have come this far and what does that show you? You have found a way to keep the group alive and that includes yourself. This has not been a fantasy, George, this has been real, the tests on your soul, on your courage and on your leadership. You have come out shining, shining like the gold you control.'

Dandelion giggles and laughs, 'Dear George, we are so lucky because you're good looking too!' Dandelion laughs again: 'Enough of me fooling around, we love you George and we have followed your miraculous journey from the old world to this one. You must now decide to take one last leap of faith into the unknown. We know you will do us proud, but we will miss you George.'

The fairies circle your head entwining and weaving around leaving a purple haze speckled with glints of gold before disappearing into the air above the hanging table. Tracy calls over to you: 'Come, George, follow us now to the courtyard.'

You follow them through a large oak door into a well lit courtyard with what looks like the sun beaming down into a swimming pool populated with butterflies. They flutter softly around, all the colours of the rainbow; some are as big as your hands and flap towards you face whilst others hover in mid air, serenely fluttering their perfect little wings. It is a joyful scene and the tropical leaves of the potted plants around the swimming pool edge are filled with different colours. You remember the last time you were here and feel a little upset, but your spirits are lifted by the innocent beauty of the papillons all around.

Hayley ushers you around the pool, 'Come on, George, we're going in here.' You enter a white, bright white, startling blinding white room with a giant velux window in the ceiling. You have been here before and immediately look towards James at the same time he has quickly fixed his glare upon you. He speaks: 'It is OK, George, I am your subordinate, we follow you now.'

With his words finishing you look up at the ceiling and the window is surrounded by thousands of bees trying to get in. You look at them quizzically and then, in that moment, you wonder why they are here.

They began to lift the entire six feet by four feet velux window from its frame and fly away. The gaping hole in the ceiling blinds you further as what you thought was the sun shines directly in towards your eyes. You look at the others as they have huddled together whilst you are sky gazing. They are intimately close. You ask: 'Err, why are you standing like that?'

Bob and Mick, who are conjoined, are followed by Tracy, Hayley and finally James. They each place their right arm fully over their own heads, placing their finger tips underneath the left side of their jaws. With an almighty crack their heads tumble to the floor and a new elongated, spheroid-shaped, grey head emerges between each of their shoulders.

The most recognisable is James' face. You have seen him before like this, with no nose and his eyes like small dots. He looks at you and says: 'Siete pronti?'

He is asking if you are ready. And for the first time you feel able to respond confidently. With power and intensity in your voice you bellow: 'Sai che sono pronto!'

You know you are ready and notice Hayley's fingers are protruding from her top. They are ugly fingers. Long, grey, wrinkly and skinny. With her hideous looking index finger she guides you towards her and you walk in time with the wiggle of her finger. As you walk forward, the others surround you.

Now in the centre of them, they all turn to you and drop to one knee. Placing their long gangly hands around your waist they lift you into the sky. It feels exhilirating. As you peer down from above them they stand up.

You trust them, but then you notice human legs falling to the floor. First it is Hayley's, then Bob's and Mick's humungously thick tree-trunk legs, then James' long and skinny limbs and finally Tracy's. You are still elevated and have not dropped. The reason for this is because, as their legs fell away from their bodies, they were replaced by thousands upon thousands of trembling, roaring, excitable bees roatating at an incredible speed.

You look below and in one breath bid the earth farewell: 'È il momento di andare.'

You rocket into the air, through the huge cavity in the

ceiling, towards the hot, radiant sun above. As you peer back down you notice the heads and bodies of your friends have merged into a golden, glistening band, radiating warmth from below. This band of gold is being thrust into the sky by jet treams of billowing bees providing raw glorious power.

The adventure has just begun.

TO BE CONTINUED...